LET ME IN
BOOK 2

Perfectly LONELY

JESSICA MARIN

PERFECTLY LONELY

(LET ME IN, BOOK 2)

JESSICA MARIN

jessica marin

Cover Design by Najla Qamber Designs.

CONTENTS

PROLOGUE

LAYLA

It was a beautiful, sunny day when I met you at college orientation.

It was a beautiful, sunny day when we got married on the beach of Sanibel Island.

It was a beautiful, sunny day when you gave me the last kiss goodbye before going out with friends on a boat on Lake Michigan.

And it was a beautiful, sunny day on the day I buried you.

As I sit here visiting your grave on the anniversary of your death, I look up at the sky to find it another beautiful, sunny day.

I feel that days like today are a big fuck you to people like me. People who have unfairly had loved ones taken from them and are expected to have dispositions that match the weather when blessed with such beautiful days. Any happiness I show the world is mostly a façade, because on the inside I am still completely gutted that you are not here with me anymore. Doesn't matter that it's been years since the last time you touched me. People say that time heals all wounds and it'll get easier, but my anger hasn't dissipated.

We were only married for two years.

We never even had our chance to have children.

Everyone says it was a horrible tragedy. An accident that no one could have predicted. You were just enjoying the lake when another boat collided with yours. Out of all the people on both boats, you were the only one who didn't make it back.

And I still want to know why.

Why were you taken from me?

What lesson was I supposed to learn from this?

Because I fell in love with you the first moment you shined that blinding smile at me. I treasured and cherished every day we were together. I was thankful for you in my life, never once taking advantage of you or our life together.

Some days, I wake up feeling like I am in a horrible nightmare. It's all a cruel joke. That I am being punished, but for what, I do not know. Instead of remembering our good times together, I am drowning in my bitterness toward a love I feel was wasted.

If you met the person that I have become since your death, you wouldn't even glance in my direction. To fill the void of your loss, I have thrown myself into work and when that is done, I drink to become numb before having mindless sex with strangers. Strangers who I hoped would make me feel again, but none of them come close to you. So I let them fuck me - the harder, the better - waiting to actually feel something again. And after it's all done, I convince myself that I imagined it all, that I would never do what I just did, until I lose consciousness from consuming too much alcohol.

But even I recognize that I am letting my life spin out of control. That moment of realization came when I was standing in line at a fast food restaurant and I caught the attention of a guy checking me out. When you were alive, his lewd stare would have classified him as sleazy. But I met his gaze, gave him an encouraging smile, engaged him in conversation and then proceeded to fuck him in the backseat of his car. As soon as he drove away, I threw up in the bushes and called my best friend, Jenna, crying hysterically at what a disgusting human being I've become. She dropped everything and met me at the apartment you and I once shared. She hugged me while I cried out all of my regrets, never once scolding or judging me. Instead, she cried with me and told me I was going to be okay.

If only I could believe her.

I know this isn't the life you would want me to lead. You tell me that every time you visit me in my dreams. Those dreams, the ones I love and loathe at the same time, because I wake up to what reality is for me now.

An empty life without you.

I stab at the angry tears streaming down my face and look behind me at Jenna sitting in her car, waiting. She always meets me here on the anniversary of your death. Despite her hatred for cemeteries, she does it for me and out of respect for you, whom she loved like a brother. She has experienced her own share of heartbreak and even though I've considered a second attempt at joining you in heaven, I've realized that she needs me more. Jenna now has a beautiful daughter and has embarked on another journey in love that will not be easy for her.

But when has love ever been easy for anyone?

Sighing, I kiss the grass above you and get up to depart. I look at your headstone one last time before I close my eyes, take a deep breath, and slowly exhale out the silent promises I make to you.

I promise to make better choices for myself.

I promise to start loving myself again.

I promise to be a better role model to Avery, our beautiful goddaughter that Jenna so crazily trusts me with.

I promise to start making you proud again, Charlie.

I turn around and walk back to the car, praying that I can keep my promises.

1

LAYLA

Present Day

"Where to, miss?" the cab driver asks, as I shut the door after entering his car. I blink rapidly to try to clear the fog of tiredness that is clouding my brain. I just got off the red eye flight from a business trip to Los Angeles and I am so happy to be back home in my beloved city of Chicago. I glance at my watch to see it is seven in the morning. I should try to get some sleep before working on my report about the trip. Instead I give the cab driver Jenna's address, deciding to spend the morning with my two favorite people. Jenna has been by herself with Avery while her boyfriend and father of her child, Hollywood actor Cal Harrington, has been shooting his latest movie in Thailand. I've been trying to stay with her as much as I can, being a good best friend and godmother by helping out during a trying time in her new relationship. But if I am being honest with myself, the real reason is because I do not want to be alone.

The first few years after my husband's death, I relished in being alone. I didn't have to pretend to be okay. I didn't have to smile when I didn't feel like smiling. I could be free to wallow in my self-pity and anger toward his death. I didn't want to see anyone and the only person I allowed in on a constant basis was Jenna. Not that I had a choice in the matter. She bulldozed her way into my life every single day after Charlie died. If she didn't see me in person, then she was constantly texting or calling. If I didn't answer her back in a timely manner, she was on my door step, especially after I deliberately overdosed on pills a couple of months after his passing. I believed my life had no meaning to it anymore, and therefore, no sense in living if he wasn't going to be in it with me. So in my drunken state, I swallowed as many Xanax as I could, chasing them down with a bottle of vodka. When I woke up the next day in the hospital, Jenna's face was the first to come into focus. She was sitting next to the bed, her thumb softly rubbing the skin on top of my hand that didn't have an IV in it. Her eyes were bloodshot and wild looking - a combination of sorrow and despair raging in them. That look still haunts me, but it was her first words to me that are on constant repeat when my thoughts turn dark:

"Don't you EVER think of leaving me again!"

I shake my head to clear the shame and guilt from the memories of that day and try to focus my thoughts on my current situation - how I hate the loneliness I feel when I am in my apartment and the disgust for my job. I work for a premium spirits and wine company in the sponsorship department. I started out as a brand manager, supplying local customers with our liquors for their establishments. Charlie and I were a very social couple, so it was fun to have him and our friends meet up at one of my client's bars for drinks after work. But after Charlie died, I needed a distraction. I applied for a position in the sponsorship department, knowing that the new job required heavy traveling to land big accounts and set up VIP parties around the country using our alcohol. It was exactly what I needed - or so I thought. I needed to get away from my apartment where the memories of Charlie were everywhere. I needed to get away from the city and especially away from the pity still deeply rooted in people's eyes. Everyone thought I was moving on with my life when they heard I got the promotion. What they weren't witnessing was my self-destructing behavior. How I created an online dating account so while I was away in other cities for work, I could pretend to be someone I wasn't. How I used alcohol and strange men to take me away from my reality.

I've been trying really hard to keep the promises that I made to Charlie at his gravesite during my last visit. The first couple of weeks were rough, with my body going through detox as I banished alcohol and started seeing a grief counselor. I decided to take time off of work and spent it with Jenna, Avery and Robert, Jenna's assistant and our good friend. They distract me from my darkness. They make me feel safe. Most importantly, they make me feel happy and loved. When I am with them, I feel like myself. But I know I can't keep relying on them to make myself feel happy and whole again. I need to be able to do it all on my own. I need to be strong enough to fight my own demons. Unfortunately, my job places me in unhealthy environments that feed those demons. This trip to Los Angeles was my first work trip in a while, so I strategically made sure to schedule client satisfactory meetings during the daytime, but there were two sponsored parties I could not ignore. For once in a very long time, I didn't want to go nor be involved in any work events. The first party I stayed at for two hours and immediately left when I felt myself wanting to drink more than one drink. The second party was more of an eye opening experience, as it seems I've created a reputation for myself when the very married and unattractive manager of the venue reminded me that the last time I was there, I gave him a blow job in the men's bathroom.

And he wanted a repeat performance.

Filled with shame and guilt, I immediately left and went straight to my hotel room where I proceeded to threw up from the realization that I'd been involved with a married man. After I composed myself, I updated my resume and started my search for a new career. The next day I woke up actually feeling good about myself and my future, a feeling I haven't had since Charlie's death. I was proud of myself for staying sober in those types of environments and not reverting to my old ways. I am excited to tell Jenna and Robert, as I know they will be relieved to hear that I was strong enough to take care of myself. They were worried about how I was going to handle myself on this trip.

As the beautiful Chicago skyline comes into view, I realize that I forgot to text Jenna that I was on my way. I pull out my phone to send her a message.

Me: Hey Hooch, not only have I already landed, but I am 10 minutes away from your doorstep. Surprise! So here's your warning that breakfast better be ready for me, little lady!

Jenna: (middle finger emoji)

I can't help the snort that escapes with my laughter as I can picture her rolling her eyes and flipping me the bird.

And for once in a very long time, I am excited to be back home.

2

LAYLA

"JEN-NA!" I scream obnoxiously from inside the shower. "Can you please bring me my toiletries?"

I stick my head out and look around her bathroom while I wait for her, marveling at the fact that she shares this tiny space with Cal, who is a large man. Granted, he has only been living here for less than a year - when he is in town - but still, he would easily take up the majority of this bathroom with his hard muscled body. Jenna was blessed by inheriting this condo on Lake Michigan from her grandmother before she got married. She remodeled it when she divorced her ex-husband, and it has been the perfect place for her and Avery. But with Cal in her life now, I can't imagine them living comfortably in this place for very long.

The object of my thoughts comes into the bathroom, confusion written on her face. "First off, can you please not scream? My neighbors already hate me from the chaos the paparazzi brings into their lives. Secondly, my shower is stocked with plenty of necessities. Why do you need your stuff?"

"I love you for trying to lead a healthier lifestyle, but I will take my toxic shampoo over your non-toxic, doesn't-do-shit-for-my-hair shampoo any day of the week," I say, giving her a sweet smile. "So please, can you get my stuff?"

She rolls her eyes and turns on her heel, mumbling about not understanding why I am showering before going to work out anyway. Being on an airplane makes me feel gross, so I always take a shower afterwards, no matter where my next destination might be, including a work out.

Jenna returns with my bag, opens it up and starts handing me my requested items. "Here are your chemically laced shampoo and conditioner. Will you be needing this as well?" She holds up my vibrator, a twinkle in her eye and an evil grin playing across her lips.

"Why Jenna, I didn't know you enjoy the smell of cum juice all over your hands," I joke, anticipating her reaction.

"Eew!" She shrieks and drops my beloved battery operated boyfriend. Fortunately it falls on the bathroom rug and not on the tile.

"Hey, be careful with that!" I protest, not wanting to make another visit to the adult pleasure store since I was just there two weeks ago.

"What is cum juice, Mommy?"

"AHHH!" Jenna and I scream simultaneously, startled by the sight of the little ninja that is her daughter. Avery has a horrible habit of quietly coming into a conversation at the most inappropriate moments. Last week she conveniently overheard Robert telling us about his recent encounter with a butt plug on one of his dates.

"I think you need to put a bell on her, Jenna," I say, as I close the shower curtain so Avery doesn't get scarred for life by the sight of my double E boobs.

"Avery, you have got to stop sneaking up on people like that!" Jenna scolds, as she quickly picks up my vibrator and throws it into my bag.

"I don't see any juice anywhere, Mommy," Avery says, as she

looks around the bathroom counters. "Is it in the refrigerator? Can I try some?"

"No, Avery, that is a special juice for adults only. Ask your daddy as I am sure it is his favorite kind of juice." I peek my head out to look at Jenna, wiggling my eyebrows up and down with a knowing smile.

"LAYLA!" Jenna exclaims angrily and I know I am going to hear an earful from her once we are alone again.

"Is that juice like the adult drinks that you and Daddy drink, Mommy? I can't wait to be an adult so I can have some too!" Avery says, with a lot of excitement in her sweet, little voice.

"I can't believe this conversation is even happening. Let's get ready for school, Avery," Jenna grumbles, trying to change the subject.

"I *am* ready for school, Mommy!" I hear Avery say as Jenna leads her out of the bathroom.

I smile and shake my head, still in disbelief that this is now Jenna's life. What a roller coaster this past year has been for her! It all started when she found out she was pregnant after a fling with Cal, who she met on a business trip in Las Vegas. Jenna never had casual sex before and was set on leading a life of celibacy after her failed marriage, but that all changed when she met Cal. I get why Jenna dusted off her vag cobwebs for him. Cal is the type of man that every species on this planet would be attracted to. Not only is he ridiculously good looking, but smart, successful, charming and has a sexy British accent. Just hearing him say 'hello' would wet any women's panties. When he expressed his interest in Jenna, there was no way she was strong enough to resist him. She agreed to spend the week with him during her time in Las Vegas. But Cal was persistent, wanting more from Jenna, who was too scared to give that to him. They lost touch and then she found out she was pregnant. Jenna reached out to tell him, but as a result of lies and deceit, he missed out on the first four years of Avery's life. Once it was revealed that he had a daughter, he worked very hard not only to be part of Avery's life, but Jenna's as well. It has been an emotional ride for Jenna, and even though I am hoping for a happy ending for her, I still carry guilt for my role in the deceit.

Because I am the reason her secret of having Cal Harrington's baby was revealed.

3

LAYLA

"Alright fearless leader, where are you taking us today on our adventure?" I ask as we leave Avery's school after dropping her off. Jenna's routine is to work out immediately after drop off and then go home, shower, and begin her work day until she has to pick up Avery. I swear, she is superwoman as I don't know how she functions sometimes with her schedule. I am useless directly after a workout.

"Hmm, I believe I need to torture you for teaching my daughter about a certain type of juice." She squints her eyes at me while tapping her fingers against her smirk as she contemplates what route to take for our walk.

"Every day with you is torture," I joke, which is the furthest from the truth.

"And yet, you keep coming back for more!" She laughs and I can't help but join her as she is right. "Let's walk along the shore today for some peace and calmness." Jenna's bodyguard, Mason, nods his head silently at her request and walks ahead of us toward the path to Lake Michigan. Cal employed Mason to be with Jenna when he's not around, especially since the paparazzi was aggressive with her when the story of her and Avery first came out.

I'm about to ask why she needs peace and calmness today when I look over at her and notice, for the first time, the purple bags underneath her eyes before she conceals them with her sunglasses. My gaze travels down her body and the looseness of her leggings confirm my suspicions of weight loss. Since it's not her busy season with her event planning business, the only reason for her stress would be the absence of Cal.

"What's going on, Jenna? You look like shit." I was never good at sugar coating my words, nor did I ever try to be.

"How kind of you to think so," she remarks sarcastically. "I am fine, just tired."

"Late night talks with your boyfriend will do that to you."

"That would be the case if I could get ahold of him."

"What do you mean?" I ask in alarm, hoping that this isn't a repeat performance of what they went through before.

"The director is trying to play catch up from delays, so they've been shooting scenes non-stop. I barely get to talk to him and when I do, it is usually in the early morning hours due to the time difference. Text has been the consistent communication since he tries not to wake me because when he is free, we are usually sleeping. But I want to hear his voice, so I tell him to call no matter what, but sometimes he is even too busy for that. Avery hasn't physically talked with him in over two weeks. They communicate by sending videos to each other."

"Has he told you how much longer they will be filming?" I ask, partially in concern for her and selfishly for me since I need to know how much longer I get her to myself.

"He doesn't know," Jenna says as she shakes her head. "They've been filming for three months already and are now in their last filming location, so hopefully soon."

Three months! I had not realized he's been gone that long already.

"Are you sure being tired is the only thing that is going on?" I probe, as we finally reach the start of the path to the shoreline.

"I don't know, Layla," she says with a shrug. "I guess I just feel lost...I have no clue what I am doing when it pertains to my personal life." She sighs and picks up her walking pace.

"Wait, what does that mean?" I ask again, feeling like a broken record with my line of questioning.

"I have never done this type of long distance relationship before and I thought I was cut out for it, but I don't think I am."

"Um, news flash, you were in a long distance relationship before or does Jax Morrow not count?" I remind her. It was only a year ago that she was dating the handsome hockey player who spent most of his time in the minor leagues during his hockey season, which was two hours away from Chicago. He would also spend his summers in Canada with his daughter from his previous marriage. Robert and I both knew this was not a serious relationship for Jenna as she barely acknowledged they were dating. When she did decide to become more serious about Jax, Cal showed back up in her life.

She stops short and stares at me, her mouth hanging open in shock. "Oh my God! How could I have forgotten about Jax?" She practically screams in hysterics.

"Jenna, is everything okay?" Mason turns back to us, his voice filled with concern at her uncharacteristic outburst.

"Oh, she's fine, Mason. She is just realizing what a cold-hearted bitch she is," I joke with laughter, but quickly stop at Mason's questioning look.

"I really am a bitch!" Jenna says and I know from the sound of her voice that tears are starting to well up in her eyes. I immediately grab her hands and squeeze them.

"Jenna, you are NOT a cold-hearted bitch. It's understandable that you would have forgotten about Jax," I reassure her in hopes to make her feel better.

"How is that understandable? I shouldn't have forgotten about him! Jax doesn't deserve that - nor did he deserve how I treated him," she says and I see her take a deep swallow of guilt as she has a quick mental trip down memory lane.

"You have a lot on your mind right now. Personally, I think we need to blame this all on Cal since he has consumed your every waking thought since his arrival."

"How could I have forgotten? Jax was my boyfriend. We had sex together!" She starts to walk again, her strides quick and angry.

"Oh please!" I say with a wave of my hand. "I don't remember most of the people I've slept with. So see, no big deal!"

She looks at me incredulously. "That statement makes me sad for you."

"Why?" I ask. "Guys can screw whomever they want and aren't expected to remember."

"Those guys are scumbags and I have higher expectations of you."

"Yeah well, you shouldn't." I huff, wanting to change the conversation away from my flaws.

"This discussion is not about me - it's about you and why you don't think you're cut out for a long distance relationship."

"You were the one who brought it up," she counters back.

"Well, my plan to make you feel better is backfiring on me," I grumble as she laughs at me. "I don't necessarily think that you can't handle long distance relationships. I think you can't handle the one you are having with Cal."

"Why would you say that?" She looks at me with confusion.

"Besides his job taking him halfway around the world, he consumes you! He is so…so alpha!" I say with a hint of disgust. I am not a fan of men who take control over their women's lives and feel Jenna is on that path with Cal. "I just feel that you're going to have to give up your life for him."

"In what way would I have to give up my life for him? He hasn't asked me to give up anything yet!"

"Yet is the keyword here! I can't walk and have a serious

conversation like this. Can we sit down for a second?" I don't even wait for a response as I plop down on the bench we were about to pass in order to collect my thoughts and breath.

"Mason, we're going to take a break," Jenna calls out to him. He gives us as much privacy as he deems acceptable which is no privacy whatsoever in my opinion. Jenna sits down next to me and we both take a moment to collect ourselves while staring at Lake Michigan.

"I'm going to be completely honest with you, because I love you like no one else." I take a deep breath before continuing. "Cal is an actor, so therefore, he is used to people catering to him and his needs. Going four weeks without seeing him is not a sustainable relationship with a man like Cal. He seems to be so intense...so needy."

"That's an interesting assumption considering you've barely been around him," she says, with a knowing look.

"He just seems to always demand your attention," I whine.

"Layla, we've barely hit the year mark together! Of course he is going to demand a lot of my attention," she says, annoyance laced in her tone.

"He moved in right away! How could you know if you even liked each other enough to move in together?" I was in complete shock when she told me two weeks after they started dating again that he had moved in. What pissed me off even more was that I was alone in my sentiments as her parents and Robert were one hundred percent supportive of the idea.

"Why should we start slow? We already have a child together. If anything, we need to make up for lost time. And Cal doesn't move slow. When he wants something, he goes all in."

"You don't even know his quirks. What if he's a slob? What if in his down time he plays video games all day long? Have you watched how he chews his food yet? Does he smack his lips together while he chews so you can see all his food in his mouth like this?" I smack my lips together, poking my tongue out as if I am chewing invisible food openly.

She stares at me with a look of astonishment on her face. "What the hell is wrong with you right now? Are you really concerned about my relationship or is this about you being worried he is going to take me away from you?"

"BOTH!" I yell, loud enough for Mason to look back at us.

Jenna sighs and takes her sunglasses off to rub at her eyes. She looks exhausted and I suddenly feel guilty for my outburst. I should have kept my mouth shut, but when it comes to Jenna, I can never keep my opinions to myself. She is my sister from another mister and I would take a bullet for her - that is how deep my love for her is.

"My relationship with Cal has not started out normal or easy, and if it was any other person, I might have not given them another chance. But Cal is different. This relationship is different. My feelings for him are completely different from what my feelings for my ex-husband were. It is a different kind of love. My love for Cal is so intense that sometimes the thought of losing him hurts like no other pain I thought I had experienced." She places her hand over her heart as if just speaking those words are causing her pain. "I don't expect you to understand, but I do expect you to respect my decisions and my relationship."

"I do respect your decisions and I am trying to respect your new relationship, but I don't want to see you lose yourself into a man. And how can you say you don't expect me to understand? I buried the love of my life!"

"I'm not saying you don't understand loving someone, Layla," she say sternly. "What I'm trying to say is that you can have different types of love with different people. You can't compare your love for Charlie versus my love for Cal. Love is love and comes in many different forms and styles."

She sighs and takes my hand. "I need you to trust that I know what I am doing with my heart. I appreciate your love and thank you for sharing your concerns with me. I just ask that you give him a chance. I really want this to work with him and I'm realizing that with his profession, I too am going to have to make some sacrifices."

I'm about to interrupt her, to tell her that is exactly what I am worried about when she holds up her hand for me to stop and looks at me intensely. "The sacrifices I have to make, Layla, might take Avery and I away to be with him while he is on location. But in no way shape or form would I EVER sacrifice our friendship - our sisterhood - for a man."

I squeeze her hand and swallow the lump that has formed in my throat. I know I should never have doubts about our relationship. I should be confident that we will always be best friends. But I have seen men come into women's lives and change the dynamic of their relationships with their friends and I can't help but be concerned it might happen to us. When Jenna was dating her ex-husband, I felt like I was dating him too, because I got to spend time with him as well. I have barely spent time with Cal and a lot of that has to do with both of our schedules. When he's in town, I am usually traveling, and vice versa. He deserves for me to give him a chance as he does make my best friend very happy.

"I'm sorry, Jenna, I just can't help but feel I'm going to lose you," I say, my voice cracking from the emotions that I am trying to hold back.

She pulls me into her and hugs me as tight as she can. Jenna always hugs the people she loves tightly, so I can feel her trying to wrap her arms around me even tighter than her usual hugs. "You are not, nor will you ever, lose me, Layla!"

We stay like this for a little longer and finally pull away, both of us dabbing at the tears falling from our eyes.

"I know you're afraid of me losing myself, but I'm more afraid for you. You have been doing so great these past four weeks and I'm scared that with Cal coming back, you'll lose your way. Please promise me that you're going to stay strong and keep working on yourself, mentally and physically?" She grips both of my hands and squeezes, forcing me to look at her.

"I promise I will try, Jenna. I will try to stay strong. And, I will try to give Cal a chance."

She smiles confidently at me and I silently pray that I don't let her down.

"Good! Now, can we please continue on with our walk?"

"Only if we can grab a donut on the way back. I need some carbs and sugar to soothe over my emotional state, as that was way too adultish of a talk at this time of the morning."

"Absolutely!" she says, surprising me with her agreement. We laugh, grab each other's hands and start swinging our arms together as we walk, exactly how we used to do as kids.

And in this moment, everything seems like it will be okay.

4

CHASE

Click, Click, Click.

The sound of the camera's shutter clicks loud and furiously as I take photos of the two women leaving the donut shop. I halt taking photos and review the shots I got of the petite brunette and her blonde friend. My focus is on the brunette, Jenna Pruitt, the girlfriend of mega star, Cal Harrington, and the mother of his child. Photos of her are still commanding a pretty penny despite the hype of their scandal dying down.

A scandal that was revealed by ME.

I sigh and slowly start to follow them, reminiscing about that day. I didn't really care back then about the consequences of what taking photographs of celebrities could do to them. I didn't give a shit if it would hurt them or their loved ones. I needed money and I needed it quickly, which is the only reason why I got into the paparazzi world. All I cared about was how many zeros those photographs would bring to my bank account. Some celebrities and their photos vary with the amount of money they bring in. What really makes the money is if you have a shred of evidence of a story that could be reportable. A story that gained interest and traction to become world-wide news. I was on the hunt for that next BIG story. A scandal that was so big that I could command close to six figures. Fate delivered that scandal right to me in the curvaceous and beautiful package that is Layla Sands, the best friend of Jenna Pruitt.

It was just last year that I was at a famous nightclub in Las Vegas to photograph another sponsor endorsed party for the latest B-list celebrity. These parties in Las Vegas are a dime a dozen. They are my least favorite events to cover as I feel I am only supporting the already inflated egos of narcissistic celebrities who shouldn't be paid to attend their own birthday party. Photographing them was a quick and easy way to make money, so when I had the time and was desperate for cash, I would attend these parties. The company that Layla works for are major players at sponsoring these type of VIP events. Despite their reputation as always putting on excessive parties to keep their vendors and celebrity guests satisfied, I had never attended their parties before. I arrived at start time to scope out the club before it got crowded, knowing that these parties always tended to start later than advertised. I was taking some shots of the club to check out the best lighting when I noticed Layla. A blind man would have felt her presence, but if he could see her, he would have seen the face of an angel and heard the voice of a sultry, seductive siren. She unconsciously commands your attention with the confidence that radiates from her. I was intrigued when I saw her, but quickly became enthralled when I heard her magical laughter.

I was determined to meet her.

I did my job sparingly that night, my intentions on meeting Layla becoming my sole focus. She was hard to get to at first, with the manager of the club sticking close to her. I placed myself in her line of vision, waiting for her to scan the crowd. I knew she would notice me because I'm a good looking guy. Not trying to be cocky about it, but years of women throwing themselves at you and telling you how hot you are will indubiously convince you so. As soon as I caught hold of those blue eyes, I gave her my best smile and saluted her with my drink. I wasn't prepared for the sexy smile she gave me in return, nor could I hide my body's reaction when she raked her smoldering eyes over me from head to toe, her return gaze showing crystal clear that she liked what she saw.

I felt like the prey about to be devoured - except I *wanted* to be devoured.

Devoured by her.

I liked her boldness. It was refreshing for once to see a woman showing she was interested instead of playing games and being coy. As soon as I saw my opening, I swooped in and introduced myself to her. It was loud in the club, so we had to be in close proximity in order to hear each other talk. Despite her luscious breasts on full display in her low cut dress, my eyes were drawn to her mouth. Full, succulent, pink lips that were the perfect lips to be kissed. Her breath was a combination of her cinnamon gum and alcohol and I was ready for a tall drink of her. Her smell was intoxicating and it took all my willpower to not claim her lips as I was dying to know if she tasted as good as she smelled.

I wanted this woman and I was going to make damn sure I had her tonight.

We started off with the usual bullshit small talk. I told her I was a photographer, commissioned to be here tonight to take photos of the famous guest of honor. Lots of women become impressed when you start mentioning that your line of work included celebrities, so I started rattling off the current major stars, implying that I have photographed them. Some of it was true - most of it was lies. As soon as I said Cal Harrington, whom I have never had the pleasure of meeting, her whole demeanor changed. She looked at me with disgust and asked if I was friends with him.

Right then and there, I knew there was a story.

After I reassured her I was not friends with him or any of the celebrities I photographed, I started to devise a plan to find out what about Cal Harrington brought out her disdain. Most women would have been begging to know what he was like, but her reaction completely caught me off guard and made me suspicious. I changed the topic of conversation and started pumping her with drinks. She greedily accepted and as the night went on, she loosened up. I snuck in my questions like switching gears when driving a stick shift and her answers started to slowly place the pieces of the puzzle:

It has been almost five years since she had been back to Las Vegas.

She was last here with her best friend, Jenna.

She hated this club as it reminds her of the heartache Jenna has endured since being here.

The heartache that Cal Harrington has caused Jenna.

She took breaks in between her story and I continued to occupy her with more liquid courage. She was getting drunk, not noticing that I switched my drinks to water in order to keep my mind clear. She wanted to dance and I appeased her to get her to feel comfortable with me, to trust me. It was there that she completely turned the tables on me and almost made me forget my new found purpose. My body came to life as she rubbed herself all over me as we moved to the rhythm of the music. Her hands made their way to my ass as she grabbed on, placing herself right against my dick, which was aching to be released from the confines of my pants. I grabbed her face, brought my lips down to hers and soon forgot who and where I was.

She tasted better than I could have ever imagined.

I wanted more.

I needed more.

I HAD to have more.

Less than 30 minutes later, we were in her hotel room, fucking on the floor as our need for each other couldn't wait for any bed. It was the breaks in between our sex sessions that I found out why she hated Cal Harrington so much:

She hates this hotel as this was where Jenna spent a week with Cal.

It was in that week that Jenna got pregnant with Cal's baby.

A baby that Jenna was told he didn't want and didn't plan on supporting.

As night turned into early morning, sleep was the last thing on my agenda as my excitement grew from the impact that this story might have in store for me. Once Layla was asleep, I reached for my phone and started researching Jenna. Google confirmed that she was in Las Vegas as the opening speaker for a women's entrepreneurial conference during the exact dates that Cal Harrington was reportedly seen around town in preparation for the movie he was shooting at the time. I needed to leave and start getting more facts to work on this story. Time was of the essence and unfortunately, my time did not include Layla. I left her a note before sneaking out of the hotel room, thanking her for the best sex of my life (which it was) and for the story that was going to make me a lot of money.

Yes, I'm an asshole.

But desperate times call for desperate measures and I was desperate.

I went straight to the airport and grabbed the first flight to Chicago that morning. I needed to see Jenna and her child for myself. The online white pages directory provided me her address and as soon as I landed, I went straight there and planted myself outside her building until I saw her. I saved her image from the bio on her website and read up on her while I waited. I was not surprised why Cal Harrington would have been interested in her. Besides being a successful business woman, she was also beautiful. I couldn't help but wonder why she hasn't gone public with the story yet. According to my research, she was dating a hockey player, but Cal Harrington was worth more money than any successful hockey player.

Why would she not reap the benefits of going public of how he won't support his own child?

My luck continued as I didn't have to wait long to spot her. I followed her from her apartment as she walked to her destination, which to my excitement was a pre-school. I positioned myself far enough away so she couldn't see me, but at an angle where I would get the best shot of her when she walked out. I feverishly pressed the shutter button as she came back out holding a child. I watched through the lens as she put the child down, grabbed her hand and started walking toward me.

I took as many photos as I could get of them before they rounded the corner, their backs now retreating away from me. I held my breath as I looked through the images I captured on the screen of my camera and zoomed in on one of the photos of the child's face.

A face that clearly resembled Cal Harrington.

She was a beautiful child, with long brown hair, blue eyes and a gorgeous little smile. I stared at her image, my heart pounding in my chest as realization started to set in that Layla was telling the truth.

JACKPOT!

I reserved a room at the closest hotel to Jenna's apartment, willing to pay the exuberant expense of hotels in downtown Chicago. I ordered room service and started writing down the tale of how once upon a time, a divorced business woman from Chicago met a famous actor on a flight to Las Vegas, got pregnant with his kid and the douchebag wanted nothing to do with either of them. Gossip magazines and news outlets all around the world will eat this story up as golden boy Cal Harrington is not quite the British Gentlemen as he likes his reputation to perceive him to be. Once I wrote out everything I had learned from Layla and my research, I picked up the phone and pitched my story to every major gossip news outlet in New York, Los Angeles and London. After accepting the highest bid offered to me, I hit the send button with zero hesitation and no regrets.

Two weeks later, I was drowning in regret.

Because within those two weeks, I met a woman who was

barely holding herself, and her life, together from the revelation of a story that was not mine to tell.

That woman was a single mother who was working her ass off to make a life for her and her child, while running a successful business.

That woman was a human being who just wanted privacy and didn't want the whole world to know who her child's famous father was.

That woman didn't want or need a reminder of the hurt from the rejection of a past lover.

That woman was now prey to the swarm of vultures in the form of paparazzi who wanted a piece of her and her child's life.

When Jenna discovered me following her for the first time, I was stunned by her fear and anger toward me, despite her not even knowing I was the whistleblower. She hated me for what I was, what I represented, and how I was the reminder of what her future of now being in the spotlight was going to be. And it was after that day, I realized what I had done.

I irrevocably changed her life.

And at the time, it was not for the good, but for the bad.

And then, at one point, for the worse.

Her disgust toward me made me feel like the piece of shit I was. As the consequences of my actions started to rear its ugly head, I vowed to make a wrong situation right by trying to protect her and Avery. I warned her about the paparazzi that were going to say vile things to her, to get a reaction from her, especially the notorious Danny Salari. I followed her every move from a distance and when she was safe in the confines of her apartment, I followed Danny and the other paparazzi to hear what their next moves for her were. With my loyalty toward Jenna growing each day, my disgust for Cal Harrington and the notion of him not wanting to be part of his daughter's life grew to the point that when he finally arrived in town to meet his daughter, I confronted him on what on despicable human being I thought he was.

Imagine my surprise to find out that he was actually a victim in this narrative.

With this new found knowledge, I agreed to his offer to pay me to watch over Jenna. He needed to know where she was at all times for her safety, especially since unbeknownst to her, a death threat was made against her and Avery. From her viewpoint, I was just another wolf in the pack of paparazzi, but in reality, I was now supplying Cal with information on her whereabouts without her knowing. It made me feel better that I now had a purpose of good, especially when her opinion of me started to soften each and every time I came to her rescue from the 'evil' paparazzi. I started to believe that I could redeem myself from bringing all the chaos into her life by protecting her. I believed the lies that I told myself every morning I got out of bed to follow her.

Because in reality, she and Cal Harrington still had no idea that I was the one that made the pact with the devil.

I kept this charade up by avoiding Layla at all costs, despite my longing to talk and apologize to her. When I wasn't following Jenna and the other paparazzi, I would try to follow Layla when she was in town. It angered me to see her get drunk and throw herself at men. I read about her husband's death when I researched her and it made her actions understandable. She was still in pain and I wish there was some way I could take it all away from her. I knew this couldn't be the normal behavior of someone Jenna would call her best friend as Jenna seemed to be the polar opposite, behavioral wise, than Layla. I wanted to save her from herself and reassure her that she didn't need to be doing what she was doing. I had no idea if Layla would even remember me from that night. I hoped she did, but I couldn't risk her knowing that I was here and revealing to Cal and Jenna that it was me who sold their story. So I kept myself hidden from her when she was around Jenna. But when I watched them together from afar one night and saw that they were in trouble, I decided that I could no longer keep running from the truth.

The silver lining in this was that Cal and Jenna got their happily ever after together because of my original actions. They have realized this and forgiven me. I am even still temporarily employed by Cal to follow Jenna and watch over her - with her knowledge of it this time. The only one who has not forgiven me is Layla. Since she has been practically living with Jenna this past month, I have seen her every day, blossoming. She is becoming healthier, her beautiful smile now an everyday occurrence. A smile that I want to see more of, preferably aimed toward me.

My time in Chicago may be running out soon and I realize now that my new mission before leaving is redemption.

Redemption in the eyes of Layla Sands.

5

LAYLA

"Can we PLEASE leave for lunch already?"

I glance up at Robert as he continues his constant whining about how hungry he is and how he wants us all to take a lunch break. I look over at Jenna in her home office, typing rapidly on her keyboard and can tell she is nowhere near ready to break for lunch. As soon as Jenna and I got back from our walk, we got ready for our day and decided to work from her home today. Her dining room used to be Robert's office/conference table, so her apartment is fully equipped with everything one would need from a regular office. Due to her company's growing success, she decided to rent a small office space downtown that she and Robert, along with two new employees, occupy. As soon as Robert heard that we were working from home, he decided to join us. We have been silently working compatibly these last two hours and I am pleasantly surprised to see that I have knocked out most of my to do list from work.

"Can you wait thirty more minutes, please?" I ask, as I try to finish my report from the trip to Los Angeles.

"You said that thirty minutes ago!" He huffs, slamming his laptop shut.

"It is only noon, Robert! Get a snack and calm down."

"I would be calm and not so ravenous right now if you bitches would have brought me back a donut. Some 'work out' that turned out to be for you!" He air quotes 'work out' and looks at me with genuine anger in his eyes. I can't hide the smirk on my face, relishing in the enjoyment of watching his child-like tantrum. "Furthermore, you've lived in this house for a month. You know the snacks that occupy that pantry. It is all cardboard, crap tasting, healthy shit!"

I laugh, as he does have a point. Since Cal moved in, Jenna's selection of snack food went from moderate on the bad for you scale to ridiculously healthy. I can't help but feel that Avery is missing out on some snacks that should be staples in her childhood.

"Wait a minute, how do you know we had donuts during our walk today?" I look at Robert with suspicion as it dawns on me that Jenna and I never mentioned our detour today. He returns an evil smirk right back and casually shrugs. I glance over at Mason to see if he has any guilt written all over his face, but like usual, he conveys no emotions. After he took a shower and got dressed, he planted himself on the couch with his laptop and has been there ever since.

"Don't look at Mason that way, he wasn't the one who told me," Robert says as Mason looks up upon hearing his name.

"You didn't tell him we had donuts today?" I question as Mason shakes his head no and goes back to his work. I roll my eyes at his refusal to use any kind of language to communicate. I've tried really hard these last six months to get Mason out of his shell, but he sticks to his sole focus of protecting Jenna and Avery and only talks when needed.

I look back at Robert, wondering if he and Mason communicate via telepathy and have decided to mess with me. "I don't believe either one of you. Mason was the only person with us."

"Au contraire, ma chérie! It's such a shame how you have

quickly forgotten about your sexy, Canadian lover," he jokes, as my mood immediately sours at the mention of Chase Wilson. I have purposely blocked that man from my mind and forgot that he still follows Jenna around, reporting back to Cal her whereabouts and copying Robert on all of his reports. It is one of my grudges against Cal as I don't like how he has her followed, despite his claims it's for her safety. What really stumps me is how he continues to employ Chase, knowing that it was he who revealed the story AND he's made money off of it. Why would he want that man in their lives still?

"Please don't ever mention his name in my presence, especially the part of any kind of relations I had with him," I demand and look Robert in the eyes for him to see how serious I am.

"You mean the part where his dick was inside of you?" he asks, raising his eyebrows in mock innocence.

"Ugh, why do you have to be so crude?" I pick up my pen and sling it at him, hitting him right in the chest. I am somewhat satisfied when he yells 'ouch!' - I honestly don't remember much of my night with Chase. I remember my reaction to him staring at me. I was shocked that someone that sexy was even interested in me. He looks like he should be gracing the covers of magazines and walking the runways of Paris with his tall, well-toned body, long caramel-colored hair and piercing hazel eyes. I push his sexy image away from my brain as he is enemy number one in my book, no matter what he looks like.

"Whatever, hypocrite!" Robert throws the pen right back at me, his aim just missing me as it hits the top of my laptop instead.

"I can hear the little beasts are out," Jenna says, as she steps out of her office. "Alright, children, let's break for lunch. I'm going to the restroom and when I return, please have it figured out where we are eating today." She turns on her heel and heads to the master bathroom.

"Aye, aye, Mom!" Robert chimes, while saluting her.

"I don't understand how she puts up with you two," Mason

mumbles. Robert and I gasp and look at him in shock that he actually spoke. Mason smiles at our reaction, closes his laptop and stands up to leave with us.

"He finally speaks!" Robert jokes as he gets up from the table. "C'mon Mason, we all know that we're your best gig to date."

"I wouldn't say my best gig...definitely the most amusing one so far."

I'm about to respond that he wouldn't know amusing if it bit him in the ass when we hear a key sliding into the front door lock. Our confusion turns into disbelief as the door is flung open and Cal rushes in. He looks disheveled in a wrinkled white t-shirt, running pants and sneakers. He drops his bags and looks around, his blue eyes wild with need as he scans the room.

"Hello," he greets us and starts walking forward into the apartment. "Where is..." His voice trails off as he catches sight of Jenna. We turn our heads to see she is standing right outside her bedroom door, her hand over her heart, mouth open in shock.

"Is it really you?" she faintly asks as I see her eyes start to water up. "Am I dreaming?"

"No, darling, I'm really here," he says, his eyes raking up and down her body as he slowly moves toward her.

"How? You never told me you were on your way!" She croaks, not being able to hold back her emotions any longer.

"It was unexpected. One of the crew got hurt, unfortunately. Director told us to take a fortnight off, so I got on the first plane home. I wanted to surprise you."

"What's a fortnight?" Robert whispers to me.

"Two weeks," Mason whispers back before I could answer. Not that I had any idea as I'm not up to speed with British jargon.

Jenna suddenly catches all of us off guard by crying out and running straight to Cal. He lifts her up and she automatically wraps her arms around his neck, her legs around his waist. She buries her face into the crook of his neck, her back shaking from her sobs. I can't contain my own tears falling down my cheeks as her cries stab at my heart. Seeing my best friend in pain is excruciating, but watching her reaction makes me realize just how deeply in love she is with him.

"Please don't cry, darling. I promise you, Jenna, we're not doing this again. Do you hear me?" He nudges her with his chin to get her to look at him. "We're not going to be apart for this long ever again. Okay?" He brushes away her tears with the pad of his thumb, wraps his hand around the back of her neck and crushes his lips to hers. Jenna tries to kiss him back, but she is so overcome with emotion that she resumes hiding her face into his neck to cry.

"Do you guys mind giving us some privacy?" Cal asks as he carries her into their bedroom and kicks the door shut. The three of us look at each other, grab our belongings and head to the front door in silence.

"Well, we know what Jenna is having for lunch today." Robert quietly says, as he closes and locks the front door. I cover my mouth to stifle my giggle while Mason shakes his head in disgust as we head to the elevators for our now extended lunch break.

6

CHASE

Harrington spotted at O'Hare.

I do a double take as I read the text from a fellow paparazzi who likes to spend his days stalking the private plane terminal at O'Hare International Airport. *What the fuck?* I have been trying to get in touch with Cal for days. He could have at least warned me that he was heading home. I quickly text Robert for confirmation and ten seconds later, he responds.

Robert: He just showed up as a surprise thirty minutes ago. He and Jenna are slapping skin right now, so don't expect to hear from him for a while.

I shake my head to clear out the mental image that Robert just provided me when my phone starts ringing in my hand. I look down to see that it is my brother, Rhys, calling…again. I have ignored his calls the last three times, but I know I can't continue avoiding him. With a heavy sigh, I sit down on my couch to brace myself for what is expected to be an unpleasant conversation and answer his call.

"Nice of you to finally pick up the fucking phone, Chase!" He growls into my ear.

"Why, hello to you too, baby brother," I respond back, enjoying getting some sort of rise out of Rhys. Rhys is known as the 'Ice King' - not only for his career in hockey, but because he shows zero emotions or feelings.

"Chase," he warns, his voice full of tension and I can just picture him rubbing his eyes like he normally does when frustrated. "I really need you to answer the phone when I call. Better yet, I need your ass on a plane home NOW!"

"Why?" I ask, sitting up in alert. "What's going on?"

"Same shit, Chase, just a different day. I'm barely keeping this company afloat. I can't do this by myself. All the potential investors we've approached refuse to have a meeting with me if you aren't going to be a part of it!"

"Why do they have to know I won't be there?"

"Because I'm not going to lie to people who I'm seeking millions of dollars from!" He counters.

"It isn't lying, per se, Rhys. Once they arrive for the meeting, you can tell them I unexpectedly couldn't make it," I suggest.

Rhys was always the good boy. Never wanting to lie or mislead people. He never got in trouble at school or at home. He knew from a young age that he wanted to play hockey so that's what he focused on. I was supposed to inherit the family company and Rhys was supposed to play in the NHL. Our father even bought a minor league hockey team for Rhys to run when his future hockey career was over with. But his dreams of getting into the National Hockey League died that day our father did.

"Unlike you, Chase, I value my honor and reputation."

I ignore his insults that are directed at my current profession because I am tired of fighting with him. He disapproves of my life as a paparazzi - hell, so do I - but it's the quickest way I can help save our family business. He refuses to acknowledge the sacrifices I am making for our mother, for him, for this company that I now don't even want to be associated with.

A company that if it wasn't for my mother's birthright, I would let go straight to hell where my father is.

I never wanted to run the family business. Owning the world's largest ice wine estate sounds pristine, but doing the actual labor of producing the ice wine is boring as shit. I used to hate being dragged into the fields as a young boy by my father, as he watched and yelled at the employees. Don't get me wrong, I have huge respect and admiration for all of our employees who harvest the grapes in the summertime, and freeze their asses off by picking the grapes off the vine during below freezing temperatures in the winter. Yes, I enjoyed the good life of the revenues my family made off of the ice wine, but that was not the division of the company that interested me. When my father wanted to be the most recognizable name in Canada, he created an entertainment division of Wilson Enterprises. He wanted Wilson Enterprises, and our wine, to be associated with every major VIP event and party in Canada. He started buying sports teams, sponsoring VIP parties, event venues and arenas. I loved the idea of growing our business and brand outside of the wine industry and that was the division I wanted to run. I went to college to study business and once I graduated, I moved permanently to Vancouver to start my internship with Wilson Enterprises. My father made sure I started from the bottom to see how hard it was to run a company. No favors were handed out to me for being the heir and oldest son to Thadeus and Lara Wilson.

We grew up privileged and lived lavishly. I didn't know any other way of life, never having to work during high school or college. Being taken seriously was an everyday battle - even to my father - and I had to prove my worth by working endless hours, showing that I was smart and dedicated to growing the company name in the entertainment industry. As the years went by and my marketing plans started turning a profit, I was finally taken seriously.

Even my father was impressed - mildly, of course. Thadeus Wilson never showed he was impressed with anyone, let alone his children. He was the face of Wilson Enterprises and loved being in the spotlight. Good looking, charismatic and hardworking, my father always made sure he was well-dressed and in shape for the public appearances that took priority over his family. He lived and breathed Wilson Enterprises and never wanted to be behind the scenes. In front and center of attention is what he preferred.

And I started to become *EXACTLY* like him.

I started to enjoy all the benefits - the riches, the parties, and the notoriety of being Thadeus Wilson's son and heir. I even threw an unforgettable party at being named one of the most eligible bachelors in Canada. Vancouver, and the good-looking women that spread their legs for me, was my very own playground. But Vancouver became not enough and I wanted to dominate all of Canada- just like my father. So I traveled more, worked harder to get our name visible in other Canadian cities and soon became more in demand than even he was. Most fathers would have been proud of their son's drive and determination to grow the family business.

Instead, mine became jealous.

I was blind as to what was coming my way. Blind, or maybe just in denial. Denial of not wanting to believe that a father would sabotage his own son. I took notice when my marketing budgets were lowered. I grew suspicious when other employees were assigned to my accounts - accounts that I hunted, pitched and won for the company. And when I was passed up twice for a promotion after pouring my blood, sweat and tears into the company, I started to investigate why.

I should have minded my own damn business.

"I need more time in Chicago, Rhys," I start up again, not ready to go back to Vancouver as I feel my time in Chicago is not done yet.

"I don't understand how staying in Chicago benefits us financially. The money that Cal Harrington is paying you to spy on his girlfriend barely covers the new equipment I need for the vineyard."

"Are you saying we're running out of money again? What happened to all the money we had left over after the sale of the hockey team?" When my father died, we had to start liquidating our assets, which included the indoor arena football team and one of the hockey teams. I refused to let Rhys sell our other hockey team - the team that he was part of. The team that he grew up with and loved. I am determined to keep it so that when this nightmare is over with, he can go back and do what he loves. It won't be as a hockey player, but as a general manager.

"Yes, Chase, we have no money! After paying employee wages and creditors, we barely have anything left. That is even after the mass layoff we did once we sold the sports teams. We were in the red last fiscal year with ice wine sales due to lower than normal productions. We won't last another year if this continues."

I suck in my breath, not prepared for this kind of news. I stand up and start pacing my living room floor. I run my hand through my hair and grip my scalp, hoping the pressure might help with any ideas of what to do to get the money to save us.

"Okay...okay. We'll fix this. We can do this." I keep repeating out loud, needing reassurance for myself and my brother.

"How in the hell do you expect us to get millions of dollars from photographs, Chase?"

"I'll start traveling more. I will go back to Los Angeles, New York...maybe even London! The money is better over in Europe." My mind races at all the places I can envision myself in, knowing exactly where to place myself to get the right kind of scandal for a bigger payout.

"I don't want any more of that blood money!" He spits out in disgust, while rage fills me at his righteousness.

"I'm busting my ass trying to save us, Rhys! What more do you want from me?" I yell, as the stress of the situation washes over me.

"I want you back in Vancouver, in your office, finding and courting investors," he commands. "You have two weeks to get your shit together in Chicago and then I expect you to come back and completely take over in the quest of saving this company. You will be the one rebranding our image. You will be the one convincing people that Wilson Enterprises is still worthy of their business. You WILL fix this mess since you helped create it!" And with that, he hangs up on me.

I look down at the now silent phone and throw it on the couch. I walk over to the mini bar and pour myself a large glass of bourbon.

One sip.

Two sips.

And then I hurl the glass as hard as I can against the floor, watching it shatter into what seems like a million pieces. I fall to the floor, my knees absorbing the impact as I scream out my frustration at what life has thrown my way.

Rhys is right that I helped create the situation that my family is now in because when I started to investigate why my father was holding me back from taking the company to greater heights, I uncovered his dark secrets.

The secret of embezzling money from the company.

It took me awhile to figure it all out, but when I did, I immediately went to our family home in Victoria, hoping to talk with him in his private office. My mother greeted me at the door and told me he was upstairs, working on budgets with the accountant.

Instead he was fucking his accountant from behind.

Everything happened in slow motion from that moment on. It was an out of body experience as I approached him, pulled him off of her and shoved him to the floor. An uncontrollable fury took over my body, making me a completely different person.

A person who was experiencing the worst kind of betrayal and hurt from his own flesh and blood.

I didn't hear his whore screaming at the top of her lungs, as my roars of rage filled my own ears, while my fists smashed continuously into his face. I didn't feel his blood splattering all over me, nor did I feel the arms wrap around me as I was hauled off of him by the house staff. All I remember was his face as he was struggling to breathe through his broken nose and mouth. I remember hearing my mother's cries and the heartbreak written all over her face when she came in and saw what was happening. And I will never forget the words I left him with before I departed.

"I hope you fucking go to hell!"

He died two hours later of a heart attack.

7

LAYLA

"You realize things are about to change, right?"

Change. A word that triggers warning bells in my head. I don't do well with change and for Robert to suggest it as imminent makes me uncomfortable. I loudly gulp down the delicious cider that my taste buds were soaking in and look at Robert with raised eyebrows. We are sitting in our favorite Irish pub, O'Malley's, treating ourselves to some cocktails and bad food due to the whirlwind of a day it has been.

"If you are referring to me winning the lottery so I don't have to work anymore, then I gladly welcome that change." I give him my best signature smirk and stuff my mouth with some French fries. It has been an emotional day starting with my conversation with Jenna on our walk this morning and then the arrival of Cal. I wish I could say I was happy to see him, but his appearance signifies the end of my alone time with my best friend. Selfishly, I am not ready to give her up yet.

"I am referring to Cal being back in town. Did you see the way his whole face changed when he saw her? He was ready to pounce on her and he didn't care who was around. It was so fucking sexy!" Robert sighs and I can't help but roll my eyes at him. Robert is the optimistic romantic - wants love for everyone and is always on the search for his future boyfriend, but Cupid's arrow keeps missing him. His last couple of boyfriends just ended up in lust, not love, and Robert is quick to cut it off if he sees no potential future.

"Why are you rolling your eyes? Aren't you happy for your best friend?" he asks incredulously.

"Of course I am happy for Jenna, but I just don't think this is a healthy relationship for her."

He narrows his eyes at me and gives me a condescending smile. "Layla, I love you and don't mean any disrespect, but with the way you've been carrying on in your personal life, you are not one to talk about knowing what a healthy relationship is."

"Exactly, and that is why I am perfectly fine being alone. But we are not talking about me, we are talking about Jenna and you asked me my opinion. I still have trust issues with Cal and I don't like how he consumes her whole world."

"Why don't you trust him? Because he is a celebrity?" Robert asks while stealing some fries off my plate.

"I still can't get over how he made decisions for her without telling her. I don't like that and think it's wrong," I say a little too loudly and with more force than I mean to.

Now it's Robert's turn to roll his eyes at me. "Layla, he did that for her safety! And he already admitted he was wrong and apologized."

"How do we know that it won't happen again in the future?" I question.

"C'mon Layla, you see how in love with her he is. He didn't give up all the times she kept pushing him away. Why would you think he would mess that up by repeating past mistakes?" He leans back and crosses his arm against his chest. "I think there is something else going on with you."

"Oh yeah? Let's hear it!" I challenge. I don't know why I am doing this to myself as Robert's intuition is usually crazy accurate.

He tilts his head and looks at me. This is Robert's signature move before he decides to unleash tough love on you. He assesses you in silence and then makes his move when given permission.

"I think you're afraid Jenna is going to stop needing you. That Cal makes her so blissfully happy that she'll forget about you. You want Jenna to be happy, but you also want her to always need you. You're afraid he'll take your spot in her life and therefore, you refuse to accept him." He leans forward and places his elbows on the table. "You are also scared that without Jenna mothering you, you will slip into your old bad habits of drowning your sorrows in alcohol and fucking any penis that comes your way. You aren't blind - you see that the looks of pity that you used to receive from your friends and family, have now turned to disgust with the reputation that you have created for yourself."

I swallow the lump that has formed in my throat from his truth and try to interject, but he raises his hand to stop me.

"You are not FINE with being alone, Layla. That is complete bullshit! No one willingly wants to be alone. It's an excuse to guard your heart from finding someone just as wonderful as Charlie was and them leaving you or worse, dying again." He sighs and grabs my hand and squeezes it. "Life is so crazy, beautiful, fucked up and fragile. But I believe that people can have more than one true love of their life. Some people are lucky to live the rest of their life with one. That is not going to be your life and you need to accept that. I do believe there is another love out there for you, Layla. You just need to start believing that you are worthy of it."

Damn him and his intuition!

"Jenna, Avery and I love you so much, Layla. We only want to see you happy. This past month, we started to see that in you. You are so much stronger than you think! We will never stop helping you, but you need to continue working on you."

"I am trying, Robert. I really, really am," I softly say, drinking in his words. The old Layla would have refused to listen and become defensive. I am learning that I don't want to go back to being the old Layla. I want to move forward. I want to be healthy. I want to be happy.

But it is so much easier said than done.

"We know you're trying, Layla. We've seen that from your actions this past month and it's given us so much hope. Of course it's going to take time and you will have some more bad days ahead. That is life. But you're not alone! You never have been and you never will be. We will always be here for you."

I can't hold back the tears that cloud my vision. I give him a small smile and squeeze his hand back.

"Thank you, Robert. Thank you for always caring. For being there for all of us. I truly don't know where our lives would be without you."

"Ah well, thank you, but it goes both ways as I don't know what my life would look like without you ladies as well. We need to thank Jenna for paying me so well that I stick around." He winks at me and we laugh at his joke. We both know he could probably make more money somewhere else, but wouldn't get the flexibility, creative freedom or the love that he gets with a boss like Jenna.

"We need to make a toast," he yells to Nico, the bartender, for two more drinks. Nico quickly gets us more cider and delivers it to us. "To you, Layla! Cheers to your determination and strength to lead you on the path of health, wealth, love and happiness!" We click our glasses together and drink.

"I've started looking for other jobs. I know my job is unhealthy for me, but I don't know if I'm ready to ease myself back into the dating world quite yet," I tell him as I put my glass down and take another bite of my food.

"Start off slow. Let's create an online dating profile for you!" He says with excitement as he claps his hands. I look at him with unease, dreading the fact that I might need to tell him I already have an online account that I used in order to find one nights stands.

"I don't think that's a good idea just yet, Robert. Let me continue working on myself for a little bit longer and then I'll consider online dating." I make a mental note to delete my current account so he doesn't see it. Robert is definitely the type of friend who would create one for you behind your back and start playing matchmaker.

I watch his eyes leave me as they fix on something past my shoulders. A slow, evil smile spreads his lips as he looks back at me. "Forget online dating. I think the perfect person to help ease you back into the dating world has been underneath our noses this whole time."

I give him a questioning look and turn around to see who he is referring to.

Imagine my surprise to see Chase Wilson staring back at me.

8

CHASE

After cleaning up the shattered glass, I needed to get the hell out of my apartment, so I grabbed my camera and decided to walk the streets of Chicago. Photography used to bring me a sense of calmness before I became a paparazzi and I wanted to see if that still held true by taking photos of the beautiful architecture that makes this city so famous. Two hours later, I feel better and find myself near O'Malley's Irish Pub. I have only been to O'Malley's once in the past and that was to do some investigative research on Jenna. The bartenders were pretty loyal to Jenna, who was a regular along with Robert and Layla, and never took my bribes of money for information on her. It has a lively atmosphere and is known for their authentic Irish food and drink. With the crap day I had, imbibing in some Jameson whiskey sounded like a great idea, so I decided to go in.

Turns out my night was about to get a whole helluva a lot better when my eyes landed on Layla Sands.

Robert waves me over and I immediately see Layla shaking her head and mouthing 'hell no' to him. If she was trying to be discreet about her feelings for having me at their table, she was doing a piss poor job at it. Somehow I doubt that Layla even cares and that makes me smile even broader at them.

"Hello Robert…Layla," I nod at each of them, my gaze lingering longer on her. She looks beautiful as always, her aqua satin shirt making her blue eyes even more electrifying. The top two buttons of her shirt are unbuttoned and I can see a hint of her sexy, creamy cleavage. Flashbacks of those luscious, more than a handful, breasts start toying with my mind and I decide it's best to keep my eyes on Robert in order to prevent my dick from growing any harder. "What are you two doing here tonight?"

"Wednesday nights used to be our nights here with Jenna, so we are just celebrating the return of Cal without her." He lifts his glass and salutes me before taking a drink. I glance down at Layla's drink to see it still full.

"May I join you? I'll buy us a round," I ask and signal for the bartender before they have a chance to change their minds.

"Yes!" Robert says.

"No!" Layla shouts at the same time.

"OUCH!" Robert yells as the table shakes from Layla kicking him from underneath. I can't help but chuckle at the sour expression on her face.

"May I?" I motion with my hand to the chair next to her, seeking her permission to sit down. I notice she tries to quickly check out my body, but does a double take when the sight of my knees catches her attention.

"Is that blood on your pants?" She moves her head down so she can get a better look before bringing her gaze back up to mine, shock registering at the confirmation. "What happened to your knees?"

"They lost a battle against shards of glass," I shrug, not wanting to bring any more attention to it.

"Why were you kneeling in glass?" Robert asks.

"I was trying to clean it up." I reply nonchalantly.

"Doesn't it hurt?" Layla asks, surprisingly showing concern.

"It did, but I like dealing with pain head-on. I believe if you can conquer it without help, it's just a reminder of how much stronger you really are."

Layla's face becomes pale and she looks from me to Robert, her eyes asking some sort of silent question. Robert just stares at me with a shit eating grin on his face and nods his head up and down. I have no idea what's going on with the two of them right now, so I salute them with my drink and down my shot of Jameson. It slowly burns down my esophagus in the most delicious kind of way and I immediately order another one.

"That's brilliant," Robert slowly comments. "Don't you think so, Layla?"

"No, Robert, I don't!" She huffs and I look at the two of them in confusion. Robert's phone dings to signify he has received a text. He glances down at his phone and screeches in surprise. He picks it up and immediately starts responding back to the text.

"How many of those has he had?" I ask, nodding toward his glass that is now empty.

"Too many," she mumbles.

"Well kids, this has been enlightening, but this heavenly human of a man that I am dating has invited me to his house to watch a movie." He winks at me and air kisses Layla. "Chase, can you make sure she gets home okay?"

"Of course," I respond.

"No, thank you!" She curtly responds back.

"A gentleman always makes sure a lady gets home safely," I raise my eyebrows at her, ready for her to challenge.

"Since you are by no means a gentleman, that doesn't apply to you." She smiles at me with all the fakeness she can muster.

"Touché, my lady," I toast my glass to her and down my second shot, the burn just as intense as it was the first time. *You deserve the pain of this burn for what you did to her.*

"For a second, I'm almost sad to be leaving this entertaining banter between the two of you, but the idea that I might be getting laid tonight wins out. Toodles, darlings! I will see you tomorrow!" He leaves a hundred dollar bill on the table and with a wave, leaves us alone.

"Check please!" Layla calls out and waves at the bartender to get his attention.

"Can't you please just have one more drink with me?" I ask, not ready for her to leave just yet. The scent of vanilla and coconut raids my nostrils as she whips her head around to look at me and I immediately want to bury my face into her neck for more.

"It's not that I can't stay - I don't want to stay. Besides, I have to work in the morning," she answers with haughtiness in her voice.

"We all have to work in the morning. Please, one more drink?" I beg and give her one of my famous boyish smiles that ladies don't resist.

"How silly of me that I forgot your line of work requires waking up and ruining more lives," she slides sarcastically. My smile immediately falls from my face and that feeling of being a lowlife scum bag, that I'm starting to believe I am, has now returned.

"Layla," I sigh out in frustration. "I know you've thrown away every apology letter that I've written to you, but I am truly sorry for my actions that night. Even though revealing their story has benefited Cal, Jenna and Avery, it was not my business to tell. I should never have told their secret and I should have never made you feel guilty or shameful. Despite what you may think, I do regret my actions that night and hate myself more than you could possibly hate me. So, for what it's worth, I am really sorry and hope one day you can forgive me."

She ponders my apology, but the mistrust in her eyes is still present. The last two years I've been roaming around not caring what anybody thinks about me or my career. But I've come to realize that I care what Layla thinks. I don't want her to hate me and gaining her forgiveness will be a step in the right direction of forgiving myself.

She's about to say something but stops herself. Instead she narrows her eyes and studies my face. She leans forward and it takes all of my willpower to keep my eyes trained on her and not the opening of her shirt. I hold my breath, refusing to breathe in another whiff of her intoxicating scent.

"Why are you a paparazzi?"

I slowly exhale and silently question whether I should tell her the truth or not. Lies would only push her away if she ever found out and if I'm seeking forgiveness, then she is owed the truth. "My family's business started to struggle and becoming a paparazzi was the only way I figured I could make quick money to help save it. Or, so I thought." I shake my head and let out a short, bitter laugh at my naiveté. Her eyebrows raise in surprise at my admission and I realize that I haven't been the subject of conversation between her and Jenna. "I am a little surprised to see that Jenna didn't tell you."

Her mouth drops open in complete shock. "Jenna knew about this?"

I briefly recall the conversation to try to remember how much I had told her. "To be fair, she doesn't know the full details. She asked the same question after I helped walk her home when she tried to outrun Mason that first morning he was her bodyguard." I can't help but smile at her stupidity that day. Thank God she wasn't hurt when she went rogue and ditched him to try to prove a point to Cal that she could handle being by herself. "I told her the exact same answer I just told you."

She leans back in her chair with resignation. "How do I know you are telling me the truth? Paparazzi are just as good at lying as actors are."

Now it is my turn to raise my eyebrows at her, wondering if she is referring to Cal. "I won't be a paparazzi for much longer and unfortunately at this moment, you don't know if I am telling the truth. You don't trust me because I betrayed your trust and I understand that. You'll just have to Google me to find out if I am lying or not," I say with a sad smile.

She continues her assessment of me, her stare breaking only when the bartender brings back the change. She leaves him a tip, puts the rest of the money back in her purse and stands up to leave.

"I am still going to make sure you get home safely. We can share a cab." I stand up as well and move my chair back into the table.

She looks at me and starts again to say something but stops herself. "You already know where I live, don't you?"

I give her a knowing look before stating the obvious. "Yes."

Her eyes widen slightly and she shakes her head before turning around and heading toward the door. I follow her silently as she says good night to the bartender and I make sure to hold the door for her as we walk out. Due to the popularity of O'Malley's, we're able to get into a taxi right away. She gives the driver her address and we drive away from the pub in silence.

I decide not to engage in anymore conversation with her as I feel the air of silence is compatible and friendly. She needs time to register everything I told her tonight. I know I'll see her again before I leave to go home and I'll just keep fighting for her forgiveness until I get it.

The cab ride to her apartment building is short. I tell the driver this will be all one fare that I will pay and ask him to wait for me as I step outside of the cab to watch her walk into her building. I decide not to follow her in order to give her space and instead lean against the cab to watch her.

"Thank you for tonight, Layla." I call out after her, wanting her to know I appreciate her for listening to me. My words make her stop before entering her building. She stays there for a few seconds, before turning around and walking back toward me. My shock at her movement makes me straighten from the cab. She stops in front of me and I am captivated once again by those blues eyes that are making me feel like she is stealing my soul. She breaks her hold over me by closing her eyes and slowly gulping. I have no idea what she is thinking but it's obvious that she's having some inner turmoil. She takes a deep breath and opens her eyes to look at me.

"I can recognize what you are trying to do tonight as I myself am trying to make amends with my past behavior. I appreciate your continued efforts to apologize to me." She stops and swallows. "Therefore, I forgive you."

"What?" I ask incredulously, not believing the words that just came out of her mouth.

She nods her head at me and squares her shoulders back. "I forgive you, Chase. The old Layla would damn you to eternal hell for deceiving me, but things happen for a reason and like you said, it did turn out for the best. Besides, I'm trying hard not to be the old Layla anymore. God knows I deserve forgiveness for my sins." Her mouth twists up in a sad smile before continuing. "It actually feels good to forgive you and I hope that my forgiveness helps you heal on whatever journey you are on to forgiving yourself as well."

As I continue to stare at her in utter astonishment, I realize that I truly never knew the real Layla. How could I from just our one night stand and from observing her from afar all these months?

I am seeing a woman who I thought was weak due to her pain, but is actually strong.

I am seeing a woman whose heart I thought was shattered, but is actually stitched up and on the mend.

I am seeing a woman who I physically knew was beautiful, but is now confirmed to be beautiful on the inside as well.

I am seeing a woman I want more of.

Without thinking, I react. I grab her arms, slam her up against my body and crush my mouth to hers.

Her lips are warm, soft and taste as sweet as candy. And although I have kissed these lips before, this time it feels different because I have zero ulterior motives.

This time, it feels like a home I never want to leave.

9

LAYLA

I can't move as my body is in complete shock from his response to my forgiveness. I couldn't even try to move if I wanted to as he has a death grip on my arms, holding me against him. Physical contact was the LAST thing I was expecting...or even wanting. His lips are firm and have the subtle taste of the whiskey he was drinking back at the pub. Being this close to him makes me feel the sculpted, chiseled muscles of his chest down to the hardness of his erection and is starting to make me ache in places I don't want to ache. If I let him deepen this kiss, my underwear will be soaked. Warning bells are going off in my head that this is a very, very bad idea.

Chase Wilson is kissing me!

This is wrong!

He is my enemy!

You just forgave him.

Make it stop!

Why haven't I stopped it yet?

Because you LIKE it!

That last comment from the little devil on my shoulder gets my hands to move up his chest and push with all I can muster, which is barely anything against his strong body. My resistance breaks his kiss and the trance that has overcome him.

"What are you doing? Me forgiving you does NOT give you the right to kiss me!" I practically scream at him, not wanting him to think I want a repeat performance of our night together in Las Vegas.

'That is complete bullshit because you do!' my little devil says.

'Do not give in to the temptation!' my little angel on the other shoulder says.

My anger gets him to remove his arms, but he still invades my personal space. "I'm sorry, I just…wait," he stammers as he runs his hand through his hair and exhales a shaky breath. "Fuck that, I am not sorry! I've been wanting to kiss you since the first time I laid eyes on you."

"Do you think I am that stupid, Chase? You think me forgiving you gives you the green light for us to have sex again?"

"No, I never thought that! Layla, you are misinterpreting what I mean." He looks around and notices the stares we are getting from the few people who remain on the street. "Can we please go upstairs and talk about this?"

"Hell no, I am not inviting you upstairs to my apartment!" I turn around and stomp back to the front door of my building, completely irritated and frustrated that men tend to think with their small heads instead of their big heads.

"Layla!" he runs past me and stops me in my tracks by blocking me from the front door. "All I want to do is get to know you better. I just want a chance."

"Why? We aren't friends and up until thirty minutes ago, you were my number one enemy! Why do you want to get to know me better? So you can try to make me trust you in order to get more top secret information to sell?"

"I just told you that I am no longer going to be a paparazzi and unless you have other celebrity friends that I don't know about, what secrets would you even have for me to sell? None!" He takes a step closer to me and runs his hands down my arms. "My intentions are pure and truthful."

I shake off his hands as his touch too distracting. "You think that I am going to believe that you are actually interested in me as a person after what you did?"

"Why wouldn't I be interested in you as a person? You're smart, funny and one of the sexiest women I've ever met. I wanted to meet you before I even knew who you were associated with. Like right now, you just looking at me as you are is making me hard. Don't you remember our chemistry that night? I have dreamt about being inside of your warmth again, feeling you squeeze around me." He runs a finger down my cheek and proceeds to rub his thumb over my lips, making me shiver despite the heat outside. "Imagined these perfect lips wrapped around my cock as you suck me off."

I gasp in shock at how my body reacts to his words and remove his hand from my lips, needing to get as far away from him as possible. "Well, enjoy that image because you sure won't be getting reality any time soon! I rescind my forgiveness!" I try to step around him, but he continues to block my path.

"Layla, sex has never been unattainable for me, so what do I need to do to prove to you that I'm not interested in just a mindless fuck? Just be friends? I can do that if you'll let me in."

I cross my arms over my chest and narrow my eyes at him. "I don't need more friends."

Damn him as he gives me a sexy smirk in response. All I want to do right now is stomp my foot like a child who doesn't get her way at the mounting frustration he is causing me.

"I am asking for two weeks, Layla, of me being your friend and doing things that friends do, like going to dinner, the movies, working out, talking on the phone."

"No way! You're not getting my phone number." I shake my head. "I don't understand what is in this for you?"

"Spending time getting to know you." I roll my eyes at the cheesiness of his answer.

"What's in it for ME?" I ask, not understanding how I would even benefit from a two week friendship.

"For you to see that people do deserve second chances, no matter what their circumstances are." He grabs my hands and refuses to let them go when I try to pull them away.

"I forgave you tonight - I know how to give second chances."

"I'm not talking about me being the one having a second chance," he says softly and I can't help but watch his eyes as he pushes a strand of my hair behind my ear. His hazel eyes return to mine and I am hypnotized by their heat and the silent promises being offered to me.

"What happens at the end of the two weeks?" I quietly ask, not knowing if I am ready for his answer.

His smile starts slowly on his lips and I see the warmth of it reaching his eyes. For a moment, I am so mesmerized by the full beauty of his face that I don't fully comprehend what he says next.

"You'll be in love with your new best friend."

10

CHASE

I woke up this morning happier than I've been in a long time. Vivid dreams of Layla filled my sleep and left me waking up with a painful hard-on. Fortunately, a cold shower and my hand provided instant temporary relief. I still can't help but chuckle at the look on her face last night when I told her she was going to fall in love with me. She stared at me as if I had grown two heads and then proceeded to laugh hysterically at me, telling me I'm a cocky bastard who is batshit crazy to ever think she would fall in love with anyone within a two week timeframe. She's right in the fact that I am a cocky bastard, but when I want something, I will stop at nothing to get what I want.

And I want Layla Sands.

I have been dreaming about her since the moment I met her and, at first, I thought her constant presence in my dreams was due to the guilt of my actions. But what I felt last night when she forgave me is something deeper. More meaningful. Something I've never felt for any other woman. I know it isn't going to be easy to win her. Her walls are thick and her hurt is deep. This will be a tough fight, but the end game is the ultimate prize.

As I leave for my morning meeting with Cal at his apartment, I decide I need to see Layla as soon as possible. I take my phone out of my pocket and send her a text.

Me: Good morning, Angel! I hope you have a great day. Meet me for dinner tonight?

I place my phone back in my pocket, trying to act calm, cool and collected when really I want to watch the screen in anticipation of her response. Five minutes later, as I'm almost at Cal and Jenna's apartment, she responds back to me.

Layla: Who is this?

Me: The man of your dreams.

Layla: Seriously, who is this? If this is one of my business clients, this is highly inappropriate and I will report you for sexual harassment.

Me: This is your new best friend and you would thoroughly enjoy and want more of my kind of sexual harassment.

Layla: How in the hell did you get my number, Chase? I am going to kill Robert.

Me: Robert is a smart man and sees we are made for each other, Angel.

Layla: Please don't call me, Angel. NO, we are not made for each other and no, I cannot meet you for dinner tonight.

Me: Why not?

Layla: I have plans.

Me: Cancel them.

Layla: NO!

Me: Fine, I will just follow you to wherever you are going and wait for you.

Layla: Friends do not stalk friends! Besides, I have to work tonight.

Me: You shouldn't be working late at night. I'll accompany you.

Layla: NO!

Me: This isn't a negotiation, Layla. I want to see you. I WILL see you tonight.

Layla: You are creepy.

Me: And you like creepy. So have a great day and I will see you later...Angel!

I can't stop smiling, despite the challenge that lays ahead of me with her. I don't know if I am going to succeed in making her develop feelings for me, let alone love. I 've only had one serious relationship in my life, in college, which felt more arranged since our families were friends. All I can do is be me and show her that I am serious, but I might need reinforcements in the name of Jenna and Robert. I just hope they think I'm worthy of her and will help.

When Cal texted me last night asking for me to come over this morning, I thought it would be the perfect opportunity to give him my two weeks' notice. The timing of this meeting couldn't be better as I can talk to Jenna and Robert as well while I am here. I put my game face on because this meeting just got more serious than initially intended.

I arrive at their apartment, the doorman waving me in since I am now on the approved list of visitors. I take the elevator up and knock once I reach the door. A casually dressed Cal opens the door and motions for me to come inside. I walk in and see no signs of Jenna or Avery, only three suitcases lined up near the kitchen.

"Going somewhere?" I ask, motioning my head towards my new findings.

"Taking my girls for a quick getaway to a remote location on Lake Michigan. We will be back in a couple of days."

"Where are Jenna and Avery?"

"I sent Jenna to the spa this morning and took Avery to child care. I will pick her and Avery up by lunch time and then we will head straight there."

"Is Robert at the office?"

Cal raises a questioning eyebrow at me. "Robert is with Jenna, also receiving spa treatments this morning. Why?"

"No reason. Just need to talk to him about something." Cal

doesn't need to know about my intentions with Layla just yet. He isn't my friend, but a client, despite his proximity to Layla because of Jenna.

"I appreciate your willingness to meet with me on such short notice. Have a seat so we can begin as I am on a tight schedule this morning." He waves his hand toward the couch for me to sit. I put my camera bag down and sit on the edge of my seat, my curiosity peaked at what he wants to say to me.

"As of today, Mason will no longer be with us."

"Why? What happened?" I ask, concern filling my voice at this news. Jenna cannot go again without a bodyguard, despite the decrease in the number of paparazzi compared to last year when she was a fresh face and a new story.

"I always knew that being the bodyguard to the partner of a celebrity wasn't what he was interested in, but I was hoping he would stay a bit longer. Nevertheless, one of his former Navy SEAL mates called him with a new opportunity that was more exciting than his current job assignment." He leans forward and looks me squarely in the eye. "When we get back from our trip, I will interview new candidates. In the meantime, I would like to hire you to watch over Jenna."

I conceal my shock at his request, as I'm the last person that should be considered for the position. "I'm not trained to be a bodyguard."

"You already scan social media posts for information on where to find the next celebrity gossip and the whereabouts of those celebrities. This time you will be looking for specific threats against Jenna, Avery and myself. You also have extensive training in Krav Maga. I think you would do just fine if your talents were called upon. Besides, this would only be until a new bodyguard has been hired, which I am hoping will be in place by the time I leave."

"How do you know about that?" I narrow my eyes at him, as I start to feel my blood pressure rise at the knowledge that he has had me investigated. Only my family and close friends know about my Krav Maga training.

"I have brought you into my life and that of my family's. Every person is thoroughly investigated before I make that decision. So yes, Chase, I know all about you. From the elementary school you attended, to the millions of dollars your father embezzled from the family company that is almost in ruins." He gives me his signature cocky smirk, leans back and places one arm against the back of the sofa and crosses his legs.

I want to punch that fucking smirk right off his face.

"What do you want from me, Cal?" I growl, wanting him to cut the bullshit and get to the point.

"I want you to be with Jenna whenever she is not in my presence until a new bodyguard is hired. If I ever feel that I need you when Jenna and I go out together, you will be accessible. When Jenna and I don't need you, I want you to follow Layla. I would like for that to start today since we are leaving for the weekend and will not need you to accompany us."

This time, I can't contain the shock that registers on my face, as I wasn't expecting Layla's name to even be brought up in this conversation. "Why do you want me following Layla?"

"Jenna is concerned about Layla and since she considers Layla a sister, then that makes Layla part of my family. Jenna is worried that Layla might slip into her old habits, since she won't be staying with us anymore due to my arrival back in town. So, I want you to follow her and report back to me on her daily routine and activities."

"And what if she does revisit her old ways?" I don't reveal to him that I already have been following her for my own selfish reasons. I want to know exactly what his plans are if she does relapse.

"Jenna and I will cross that bridge if it comes to it. I am hoping it doesn't, as that will upset Jenna greatly."

I ponder what he has just asked of me, delaying telling him

that I have to depart Chicago in two weeks. This would be a perfect opportunity to get closer to both Layla and Jenna, with the possibility of persuading Jenna to help me win Layla's heart.

"How much?" I demand, referring to the price he is going to pay me for my services. Everything comes with a price and I'm not going to work for free for Cal Harrington when I should be spending all of my time trying to help save my family's company.

"I will pay you $75,000 for the next two weeks and will consider becoming a private investor in your company. I expect a tour of your offices and vineyard before I leave to go back to Thailand."

"How the fuck do you know we're looking for private investors?" I ask in disgust, wishing he didn't know such personal information about me.

"You of all people know that money can buy you any kind of information, Chase." He looks at me with a knowing smile and stands up, signaling that this conversation has come to an end.

Karma, you're a fucking bitch!

I stand up and follow him to the front door. He opens the door and like a dog obeying their master, I walk out and turn to look at him from the threshold.

"I expect your acceptance when I return on Sunday. Have a great weekend." And with that, he slams the door in my face.

I stare dumbfounded at the door, not quite understanding how I should feel about what just transpired. I am upset over the fact that he knows about the trouble Wilson Enterprises is in, but I am intrigued about what his motives are for possibly even considering being an investor. As I move swiftly toward the elevator, I realize that this might buy me more time in Chicago with Layla.

And the possibility of saving my family's company.

As soon as I get back outside, I call my brother, who picks up after only one ring.

"Get things ready, Rhys. I just secured our first meeting with a potential investor."

11

LAYLA

How dare Robert give Chase my phone number without my permission! I've blown up his phone with obscenities, but haven't heard back from him since he's getting treated to a morning at the spa with Jenna, courtesy of Cal. He is so lucky that Cal asked me to meet with him this morning, otherwise I would silently barge into his spa session and make sure the hot stones they are using on him burn the devil out of his skin. He needs to stop meddling into people's lives as I don't want Chase Wilson in mine. I forgave Chase and I want to move on.

I cross the street to Jenna's apartment and do a double take as I get closer and recognize the handsome figure of Chase outside of her building. He is talking on his phone and his body language is screaming that it isn't a good conversation. Even with his animated features, the man is ridiculously hot. Today he's dressed up more than what I've normally seen him in. He's wearing a white button down shirt, navy chino pants with a tan belt and tan shoes. Aviator sunglasses shielding his eyes and his stylish leather camera bag crossing over his body. He rakes his free hand through his hair and I find myself trying to remember if his hair feels as silky as it looks. There are girls who would kill to have his type of hair.

I shake my head at how he looks like he can be a model in a Hugo Boss ad and I can't help but wonder what in the hell his true intentions are with me. By no means do I think I am ugly, but I have curves in places he has probably never handled on his previous conquests. It makes me even more suspicious as to what his motives are since his looks are in the same caliber as Cal's looks - meaning he can get any woman that crosses his path.

I quickly look around to see if there is any place I can hide and watch him from afar, but since there isn't, I have no choice but to walk past him. Sighing in defeat, I make my way toward him as slowly as I possibly can. *Maybe he will be too busy yelling at whomever he is on the phone with to notice me?*

As soon as the thought leaves my mind, he turns toward me and a slow, salacious smile forms on his lips. My traitorous heart starts to beat faster at that smile and I am immediately put into a bad mood, not wanting to react this way toward him. He tells whomever he's on the phone with that he will call them back, hangs up and puts his phone back in his pocket. He walks the remaining distance toward me until we are standing right in front of each other. I will myself to look anywhere else but at his face.

"What a vision my eyes behold. See Layla, fate wanted us to see each other today." The words flow so smoothly from his mouth that I wonder if he majored in the Art of Seduction 101 in college.

"More like a coincidence, Chase."

He cocks his head to the side and my eyes catch sight of him unconsciously licking his sensual lips. "Is it though, Layla? I think we do have someone watching over us, wanting us to be together."

His husky voice and words make me shift uncomfortably as images of him naked, kissing down my body suddenly appear. I don't remember much from our tryst in Las Vegas, but the more I'm around him, the more my body is starting to remember.

And it's starting to demand more.

"Why are you over here and not following Jenna?" I force the unwanted mental images aside and change the subject.

"I needed to meet with Cal. Why are you here?"

"To ask Cal to fire you so you will stop stalking me." I try to give him my most serious look, but it's hard to keep a straight face when he starts laughing. His laughter starts out as a deep rumble in his chest before exploding out. It's infectious, making me want to laugh with him.

It is also damn sexy and makes me want to kiss him.

Not liking how I am reacting toward him, I try to side step around him, but he just moves along with me and places his hand against my cheek. His touch sends a shockwave of warmth through me and freezes me in place as he moves that same hand down and cups the side of my neck. He pulls me closer to him and leans down, his breath tickling my ears.

"I see the way your vein rapidly pulses when I touch you, Layla. Your presences does the same to me." He lifts up my hand with his free hand and places it against his chest. I gasp as I feel his heart ponding the same way mine is.

"This is only the beginning of how I want to make you feel when you are ready to give yourself to me," he seductively whispers in my ear and I try to swallow the saliva that wants to drool out of my mouth over how his words make me burn. I inhale his delicious peppermint breath, which causes me to look out of the corner of my eye at his lips. I almost moan out loud from the proximity of his mouth and the want of sucking on those invitingly firm lips.

If you move over just an inch, you can taste them for yourself.

Before I have a chance to even consider if I want to make that move, he stands up straight and presses his lips to my forehead. "I'll see you later, Angel," he says and walks away.

I close my eyes and take a deep breath, willing my heart to stop beating so fast. I take a step forward only to come up short by the uncomfortable wetness that has now formed in between my legs.

That man has just annihilated my panties.

12

LAYLA

I don't even give Cal the chance to say hello as I race into their apartment the minute he opens the door, mumbling that I need to use the restroom. I run straight to their bedroom and find the extra clothes that I keep stashed away in Jenna's closet. I groan out a sigh of relief when I put on a pair of new, dry underwear. I find a plastic bag underneath Jenna's bathroom vanity to use for my wet ones and stuff the bag in my purse.

Damn that man for turning me into a flustering idiot!

I come out of their bedroom and slam the door closed. I can't hide the emotions that are playing on my face as I try to calm down. Anger and embarrassment course through me as I see Cal watching me with concern. I must look exactly like how I feel.

"Is everything all right, Layla?" He asks softly, as he hands me a glass of water. I nod my head thanks and down it in a couple of gulps. I place it on the kitchen counter top, take a deep breath and look Cal straight in the eyes.

"I want you to fire Chase Wilson," I demand.

He narrows his blue eyes and gives me a questioning smile. "And why should I do that?"

"Because he's stalking and harassing me." Cal's eyebrows shoot up in surprise and I see a quick flash of anger appear in his stare before he replaces it back with his usual look of calmness.

"Can you give me some examples?"

"He's showing up at places uninvited and he keeps texting me."

"How did he get your phone number?" He gives me a quizzical look.

"Robert!" I say with such disgust that Cal's lip twitches with a smile.

"And how many times has he shown up uninvited?"

'Well...only once, but then he followed me home when I told him I didn't need an escort!" I quickly say, trying to emphasize the point that he followed me home uninvited.

"Interesting," Cal says slowly. "You mentioned he was harassing you. Has he been saying inappropriate things to you?"

Yes!

"No," I answer.

"Has he been sexually harassing you?" Cal's tone turns serious.

Technically, yes!

"N...No," I stammer, but can't hide the blush that creeps up on my cheeks from the memory of his words this morning. Cal, being the perceptive person that he is, studies my face and notices my new shade of color.

"Hmm," he murmurs. "Very interesting."

"Stop saying it's 'interesting,'" I growl, as I make air quotations with my fingers. "It isn't interesting, Cal, it's giving me anxiety. I don't want this man in my personal life!"

He assesses me in silence as he sits down on one of the bar stools. "Okay, I will talk to him, but I cannot fire him yet. As of this morning, Mason is no longer with us and I need Chase to step in for him until a new bodyguard is secured."

"Chase is nowhere near qualified to keep Jenna and Avery safe!" I exclaim in frustration, not even commenting on the departure of Mason. Not only is Chase not suitable for the job, but that means I would be seeing him more often.

"I first thought the same thing, but then I had him investigated. Do you know how a paparazzi - a good one, that is - finds their leads? Besides having the right connections and spies in place, they have to do an immense amount of research on their subject, as well as the detective work, especially scouring social media for any potential leads. This is very similar to what bodyguards have to do. They read every comment on social media, news articles and blogs to see how people are talking about the people they are protecting. They have to be on the lookout of anyone voicing imminent threats. It is all quite fascinating, really."

"But what about physical training? Has he been to bodyguard bootcamp to do whatever they go through in order to learn how to protect people?" I question, as Chase doesn't have the body-building muscles that Mason has. Chase's physique looks more like the statue *David* from Michelangelo - lean, sculpted and made for the runway.

"Funny enough, they do have bodyguard bootcamp, but while Chase has not been trained in the art of being a bodyguard, he does hold a black belt in Krav Maga training." My mouth drops open in shock as Cal tilts his head and gives me a funny look. "Have you not done your own research on Chase yet?"

"Why would I need to?" Even though I haven't yet, it doesn't mean I haven't been curious about his past and why he sought out the industry he chose to go into. Maybe I am scared at what I will find. Maybe it will change my opinion of him. "Besides, what Google tells me is not the same as what a private investigator would tell me."

"Maybe not, but you should always look into everyone that shows interest in you, Layla, even if it is just typing their name into Google." Cal gives me a knowing look as if I am child.

"I am not you, Cal. Strangers aren't actively searching me."

"Yet a stranger revealed one of your biggest secrets," he counters back with a smug smile on his face.

I grit my teeth from saying something to him that I might

regret later. I hate being reminded of my actions of that night, despite the outcome turning out in their favor.

"Enough about Chase as he is not the reason I asked you to come over today without Jenna being here." He motions for me to sit down on the couch and a feeling of dread starts to creep in. I don't like being here alone with Cal, especially if it is to talk about Jenna.

"I still get a sense of mistrust from you that I would like to discuss and get out in the open."

Ugh, so not in the mood for this kind of talk.

I look down at my hands and nod, but no words form as revealing to him why I mistrust him will just show my own insecurities.

"Despite your continuous guilt with telling Chase what transpired all those years ago, I wouldn't be here if you hadn't. So I am forever indebted to you for that."

He has said this to me many times before and I should be relieved for his gratitude, but I still can't unload the lingering shame of how my telling her secret removed all of the luxuries of a normal life Jenna used to have. Jenna forgave me right away and I know I need to let it all go. Charlie would have been mortified at me talking to a stranger about someone else's personal life if he was alive, but then again, I wouldn't have been sleeping with another man either.

It's all Charlie's fault - just like everything else that has gone wrong since his death.

I try to focus my attention back to Cal as he continues talking. "Jenna considers you a sister. Her parents consider you another daughter and Avery thinks the world of her Aunt Layla. You are important to all of them, which makes you important to me." He leans down and the movement forces my eyes to him. "Layla, I want you to be able to trust and confide in me. Not like you do to Jenna, obviously, but I want you to know that one day I hope you will feel like I am your family too."

His words are making me feel mortified for my doubts about him, but I still don't know the real Cal Harrington. All I see is him in alpha mode around her and it drives me crazy how Jenna accepts it. Their relationship is theirs, but at the end of the day, Jenna is my best friend and I just don't want to see her get hurt again.

"I appreciate those words, Cal. I am trying really hard to set the past in the past and move forward. I'm not used to seeing Jenna in such an intense relationship and well, it just makes me worried for her that she's going to get burned by you, especially since you're an international movie star with women throwing themselves at you."

"All Jenna has to do is say the word and I would give it all up for her."

I can't help but roll my eyes at him, a little disgusted that he thinks his dramatics will work on me. "C'mon Cal, you know she would never ask you to do that. Be real with me and none of this actor bullshit."

"You think I am acting right now?" He looks at me incredulously. "Layla, I am not trying to bullshit you to make myself look good. Jenna and Avery are my world and I will do anything to make them happy."

"Leaving them for months on end will not make someone happy," I spit out, not able to contain my bitterness at his profession.

"I understand how hard these last three months have been on Jenna - it has been hard on me too," he says and I shake my head at him, a look of disbelief on my face.

"Layla," he says with an unsteady breath, trying to stay composed. "I am not the enemy here. Just because you have had her longer in your life does not mean my love for her is any less."

We stare at each other in silence, the internal battle we wage against each other showing through our eyes. He rakes his hand through his hair, stands up and turns to look out the window at Lake Michigan.

"I am going to ask Jenna to be my wife when we are away this weekend. I was really hoping to have your approval before I did."

His words should not have been such a shock to my system, but yet I couldn't help contain my quiet gasp. I wasn't prepared to hear this today. Hell, I wasn't prepared to have any of this conversation today. But this should not be about me and my feelings on Cal. This is about Jenna and this is the man she is madly in love with. I don't doubt his love for her or Avery as I have never seen someone love another person as fiercely as he has shown he loves them. I need to trust Jenna when she says she won't ever stop loving me due to her new relationship. It's time to put my big girl panties on and support the people I love.

"Do you have a ring?" The words come meekly out of my mouth. He turns around, hope shining in his eyes as he nods yes. He goes into the bedroom and comes back out with an expensive looking black box. I open the box and tears immediately spring to my eyes at the beauty of the ring. Cal's taste is timeless and exquisite and it's apparent that he has been paying attention to Jenna's sense of style. The center stone is a huge emerald cut diamond and on each side of it, tiny diamonds form into the shape of a small heart. I swallow the lump in my throat and give him a teary smile.

"I approve Cal - of the ring, and of you," I say as confidently as I can muster in my current emotional state. "And as your future sister, I must warn you though that I don't think she's ready." The smile that appeared on his face seconds ago from my approval falters with my last words.

"Why do you think that?" He whispers, hurt starting to radiate from his eyes and I immediately regret what I said.

"I just think she needs more time to get back to being confident with the relationship again. This month without you was making her doubt everything."

"She was going to break up with me?" He asks in shock.

"I don't think so. She never said that," I say, flustered, wishing I kept my big mouth shut. "All she said was she didn't know if she was cut out for this kind of a long distance relationship."

He lets my words sink in and nods his head. His look of defeat is killing me and I feel like a complete bitch. *Dammit Layla, why couldn't you keep your opinions to yourself!* He sits back down on the couch with a loud sigh and I start to panic on how to make this situation right. I just probably ruined his whole vacation that he hasn't even gone on yet! He is going to be a moody son of a bitch when he picks up Jenna and Avery. Poor Jenna won't even know what hit her! I need to fix this quickly and the only way is to be completely honest with him.

"Cal, I honestly don't believe for one second Jenna is going to break up with you over long distance. She is madly in love with you. I just think she hasn't figured out how to handle when you are gone for so long. I could be completely wrong about her saying no to you this weekend if you propose." He looks at me and I see a glint back in his eyes. "You can definitely still try - I just didn't want you to be completely blindsided and hurt if she does say no."

"Thank you, Layla. I will think about it." I see his smile reach his eyes and know he is being genuine.

"Don't give up on her if she does say no. Just know that she might need a little bit more time."

He nods his head and I decide that this should be the perfect time to leave. He stands up the same time I get up to walk me to the door, but my inner voice stops me, screaming at me to ask him one more crucial question that would affect if I will truly see him as family.

"Do you plan on taking her away from me forever?" I say quickly, holding my breath for an answer I may not like.

"Chicago is our home, Layla. We might have to leave for a couple of months here and there as I want my family with me when I am on location from now on, but we will always end up right back here."

"Oh, thank God!" I rush at him, the emotion to hug him too overwhelming to ignore. His strong body absorbs the impact of my abruptness and he embraces as tightly as he can. And as I continue to cry into his shirt, completely soaking it with my tears and snot, I realize that I needed this just as much as he did.

"If you break her heart, I will pay all the money in the world to hire someone to kill you."

His chest vibrates with laughter underneath my cheek. He lets go of me to get a tissue from the kitchen for my tears. I look up at him as I dry my eyes and give him a genuine smile.

"I would be disappointed in you if you didn't." He smiles right back at me and gives me one more hug before I depart to start my work day. As I take the elevator down and exit the building, I reflect on what just transpired with Cal. He didn't have to ask why I wasn't warming up to him. He didn't have to ask for my permission to marry Jenna. Some guys couldn't care less if their partner's best friend likes them or not. But for Cal to take the time to care, to tell me he thinks of me as family and is asking for my permission for her hand, makes me realize that he's a good guy and truly is in love with Jenna. While I went into this meeting with dread, I came out of it feeling hopeful that Jenna has finally found her forever.

And I hope she proves me wrong by saying yes to him.

13

CHASE

His hands go for my neck and I manage to throw his arms out and land a punch to the stomach. He recovers quickly and I am about to throw a leg kick to his side when he grabs my leg and spins, forcing my body to go airborne and twist. I face plant into the mat with a loud thud. He places his knee into my back and leans down, both of his hands keeping me to the ground.

"Your head isn't here and you are about to get hurt. Get out and go for a run to clear your thoughts," my Krav Maga trainer says as he gets off of me. I flip onto my back and take some deep breaths, trying to get as much oxygen back into my body as I can. He holds out his hand for me to take and helps me up.

He's right, I shouldn't be here right now. I am mentally all over the place due to the phone call with my brother and should have known better than to try to train if I wasn't going to be one hundred percent focused. I enter the locker room and get my running shoes. After putting them on, I lock up my belongings and proceed to go for my run. I head straight east, pounding the pavement and running as fast as I can until I run through Millennium Park and reach Lake Michigan. My lungs are screaming in pain and I slow my run down to a walk and continue on Lake Shore Drive. As my breathing finally starts to settle back down, I reflect on the conversation with Rhys.

At first, he was adamant that we should not consider Cal as an investor due to my current history with him. He feels we need to focus on the people who are already established in the industry, but my argument back was that we could use a celebrity endorser, like Cal, which can then lead to other endorsements from celebrities, and possibly open up more doors on the international scale.

"I don't understand why you want to stay connected to Cal Harrington," Rhys questioned.

"It's always good to stay connected to high powered celebrities, Rhys. If he's interested, why should we turn him away?"

"I think there's something you aren't telling me. We have to be one hundred percent honest with each other. It's only you, me and Mom in this together. Everyone else wants to see us fail. So please, tell me the real reason why you want to stay connected to Cal Harrington." Rhys could always see through people's bullshit. Even though I wasn't bullshitting him about having Cal as our celebrity endorser benefitting us, he was right to assume that was not the only reason.

"Fine, it's because of Layla," I finally admitted to him.

"Who's Layla?" Rhys asked, annoyance in his voice present from the knowledge that I am still here for a woman.

"She's the one I slept with that night in Las Vegas - the one who told me about Cal and Jenna."

"Jenna's best friend? The widower? You are staying there to try to sleep with her again to get more information out of her?" He then proceeded to laugh in a bitter, mocking way. "Are you fucking kidding me? Wow, you really have reached a new low, Chase."

"No, I genuinely care about her, Rhys. The more I'm around her, the more I see what an incredible woman she is. I'm falling for her." I admitted and this only seemed to make him laugh harder, which in turn, made me livid. "Fuck you, Rhys! You don't know shit about my life here! You haven't been in my shoes, nor have you even met her, so stop making judgments."

"You aren't fooling anyone, Chase! You aren't in love with her. You might be in lust with her, but it isn't love. You're convincing yourself that you're in love with her, when really, you still feel like the deplorable human being you were for doing what you did to her. You still feel guilty and that's what you are confusing with love."

"No, you're wrong, Rhys!" I yelled into the phone.

"Leave her alone, Chase! Get your head out of your ass and get the fuck back to Vancouver!" And with that, he hung up on me again.

As I sit watching the calmness of the water of Lake Michigan, I wonder when my brother got to be so bitter. While he was the quiet and emotionless one, he was never bitter. I know being at the helm of Wilson Enterprises is doing this to him.

YOU did this to him!

Your lack of stepping up and not facing your rightful place in the family has made him bitter!

I groan and hold my head in my hands, as his words keep playing through my head like a broken record. I know I need to go home. It's the right thing to do, despite my reluctance. And it isn't because of the beautiful woman I'm trying to pursue here.

I don't want to go back to the desolate offices of Wilson Enterprises.

I don't want to see the hopelessness on the faces of the remaining employees.

I don't want to see the hurt that is still evident in my mother's eyes from my father's betrayal.

I don't want to see the coldness and hatred in my brother's eyes at me for leaving it all on his shoulders.

The list of reasons to not want to go home are continuous, but I have to stop running. I will go home, but before I leave, I will accept Cal's offer to watch over Jenna and spend my remaining free time with Layla. With my decision made, I start heading back to the gym and decide to call her while I walk back.

"I'm still working, Chase," she says, as soon as she picks up.

"Ah, you programmed my phone number so you know it's me when I call. Progress!" I boast to her.

"What do you want?" She asks, but I can hear the smile in her voice.

"What time are you getting off of work?" The need to see her in person is so strong that I'll go wherever she is just to see her face.

"Hopefully not too late as I'm tired. Why?" She asks, suspicion laced in her voice.

"It has been a trying day and I was hoping I could see your beautiful face to cheer me up. I can come to wherever you are for a drink. Will you have just one drink with me?" Silence is her answer back and I start to think we got disconnected.

"Layla?"

"Okay Chase, I will have one drink with you tonight. I'll text you the address of the bar to meet me at once I'm done with my last appointment."

"See you soon, Angel." I hang up and start to run, not wanting to be late for my very important date.

14

LAYLA

I sent Chase the address to my last meeting for the night, which is at a posh rooftop bar on the top of a boutique hotel in downtown Chicago. For a Thursday night, the bar is crowded with young professionals starting the weekend off early. I sit at the end of the bar and sip on water, waiting for his arrival. I know exactly the moment he arrives as I see numerous females turn their attention toward the entrance. I watch in wonder as Chase ignores all of the beautiful women he passes in search of me. When his eyes find mine, I feel their spark and the heat of his smile radiates throughout my body. My heart starts to hammer harder in my chest as he makes his way to me and I realize that I am actually excited to see him.

And I'm one hundred percent completely sober.

As Chase reaches the seat I saved for him, I push down my usual feelings of guilt for being interested in someone other than my husband. I take in his attire of a thin hunter green V-neck sweater, charcoal pants and black ankle boots. His hair is wavy from air drying and he has a day's worth of stubble growing. My hunger for dinner has now changed to a different kind of hunger.

You are doing nothing wrong, Layla.

Charlie would want you to move on.

It is just one drink with a friend.

"Hello, Angel," Chase says in his seductive voice and kisses me on the cheek, lingering longer than a friend normally would. I can't stop from inhaling his scent, the smell of his cologne making me cross my legs from the tingling sensation that he evokes from me.

Friends don't react that way toward friends.

"Hello yourself," I respond back and smile fondly at him. He sits down next to me, moving his chair as close as it will allow him to be.

"Is this place one of your clients?" He asks, as he takes in the speakeasy style decor that makes this bar so unique.

"Yes, it is. The owner and manager are very nice. They are probably some of my favorite clients to work with."

"Very cool. I like this place." His gaze is appreciative as he examines the light fixtures above our heads.

"I thought you might," I say, as I signal for the bartender to come take our drink order.

"See, you know my tastes already," he teases with a sexy smile.

"No..."I say slowly as I take a look around, "this place just looks very masculine." He chuckles at me and I grumble, "what, it's true," not wanting to state the obvious with the dark decor when the bartender arrives. I introduce Chase and we place our drink orders.

"How was your day today?" Chase asks, as the bartenders leaves to make our drinks.

"Tiring, but really good," I respond as I recall my meeting with Cal and how much better I feel about him.

"What did Cal say to you in your meeting with him?" He asks as if reading my mind.

"That is none of your damn business!" I retort, shocked at his audacity for asking.

"Did he mention me?" A flirtatious smile plays on his lips. "He did, didn't he?"

"We had more important things to discuss than you!" I lie, hoping it sounds more convincing than how I feel. I need to steer this conversation in a different direction to avoid any more of his questions. "So, you mentioned today was a bad day. What happened?" I ask, as I twist my body to turn to face him and give him my attention.

"Just an unpleasant conversation with my brother," he smiles tightly at me. I raise my eyebrows at him, signaling that I am waiting for more. He stares at me for a couple of seconds longer before sighing. "Things at home are not very warm and fuzzy right now."

"Why is that?" I ask, wanting to hear more.

"Because when my father unexpectedly died, I should have taken over the family business. Instead, I ran away like a coward and left it all on my brother's shoulders," he says, his tone bitter.

"So, go back and help him," I suggest, not fully understanding why he is making this sound difficult.

"I wish it was that simple," he says, before taking a big gulp of his drink that the bartender put down in front of us.

"Why can't it be that simple?" I counter, wanting to hear what his excuse is.

"My mother and brother hate me."

I look at him skeptically. "Why would they hate you?"

"Because I killed my father." He looks me straight in the eyes and downs the rest of his drink.

I stare at him, not believing the words that just came out of his mouth. There is no way he would be sitting here with me if he truly killed his father in cold blood. I scan his face a little harder and see how tired he is, along with something else in those turbulent eyes.

Pain.

I shouldn't care about what is going on in his personal life. I should be staying far away from him and concentrating on my own self-healing. But I can't ignore the hurt that he can't hide when talking about his family. I don't like to see it. I don't want to see it.

"This isn't an appropriate environment to have this conversation. C'mon, let's go back to my place." I reach for my purse to extract my wallet to pay the tab.

"You're inviting me back to your place already? But we just got here." Chase says in mild shock as he places two twenty dollar bills down for the bartender before I could even get my credit card out.

"Yes, but you are coming over as a friend with ZERO benefits," I say firmly, making sure that he understands that there will be no sex in store for him tonight with me. "We are just going to talk."

"Looks like there was a silver lining to killing my father after all," he jokes as we get up to leave.

"That's not funny and I don't believe you!"

"It's true, Layla, so if you don't want me to come over, say the words now." I look at him before answering, the warning bells in my head going off at full blast, screaming that this is a bad idea. But, I can't ignore that haunting look of despair and pain that I see in his eyes.

The same exact look that stares back at me from my own mirror.

Part of the healing process is forgiving. I forgave this man and now I want to help him.

"Let's go!" I command as I grab his hand to lead him out of the bar to my apartment.

15

CHASE

Talking about my family problems is the last thing I want to do. Especially with how fucking delectable Layla looks in her work attire. Her clothes seem simple enough of a black dress shirt with a red pencil skirt and black heels. It is perfectly tailored to her body and makes my imagination run wild with what kind of lingerie she might have underneath to match the sexy appeal of the overall outfit. She kicks off her shoes as we enter her apartment, giving me a glimpse of her painted red toenails while my eyes trail up to watch her sexy calf muscles work as she walks ahead of me.

God bless this woman as I want to lick every inch of her.

I need a distraction or else I won't be able to refrain from taking her on the couch. Sex right now would be quick and rough as my mood is feral due to the roller coaster ride of emotions my family has me on. I haven't had sex since Las Vegas and spending more and more time with her has made pleasuring myself insufficient. I start to look anywhere but at her, trying to focus my mind on the decor of her apartment and not the ache of my cock.

"How long have you lived here?" I wonder, as the apartment is modern with hard wood floors and an updated kitchen that has industrial type hardware and lighting. I am quite surprised, as this seems to be opposite of her feminine style.

"Ten years," she says, as she busies herself with opening up a bottle of wine and pouring us each a glass. Ten years means this is the apartment that she shared with her husband. The thought quickly works its magic on deflating my hard-on. The walls are void of any décor, but as I take a closer look, I notice nail hooks with scuff marks from a frame. It seems what once were reminders of her husband have since been taken down.

"It's a nice place," I say, as I walk to the balcony and admire her view of the city. "How many bedrooms is it?"

"Just one," she replies as she comes around the kitchen island and hands me a glass of wine. "I think it's time for a change though."

"Oh yeah? Why?" She swings her hair behind her shoulders and the action makes me picture my hand wrapping the golden silk in my fist and pulling her head back as I pound her from behind. I grip the wine glass harder and try to blink my carnal thoughts away.

"Too many ghosts here," she smiles sadly at me, which makes me regret even asking.

I hold up my wine glass to her to make a toast. "To change," I say and we clink our glasses together. I take a long pull of the delicious wine while my eyes stay locked onto hers. I savor the flavorful liquid as long as I can and make a loud gulp as I watch her tongue dart out to lick the remnants of wine off her lips from her sip.

"Are you hungry? I'm starving!" I hastily say, hoping she didn't notice my voice a higher octave than normal. She gives me a questioning look and I immediately head to the kitchen to distract myself. "I can cook us dinner if you have food."

"You know how to cook?" She asks skeptically, as she follows me into the kitchen. I open up her refrigerator and am relieved to see she has recently been grocery shopping. "Yes, my mother taught my brother and me how to cook our family meals every Sunday when growing up. Do you like to cook?"

She wrinkles her cute nose in disgust. "No, I like to pay someone to cook for me."

"Then why do you have all these groceries?" I chuckle, as I get the pans out from underneath the cabinets and take the food out that I want to prep.

"I bribe Robert with free food if he will come over and cook it for me. He's actually a good cook."

I laugh at her resourcefulness and start cooking the chicken I found in the refrigerator. She watches me intently as I describe what I am doing so she can see that this is easy enough for her to cook by herself. Thirty minutes later, we are sitting down at her dining room table, our plates filled with grilled chicken, asparagus and couscous.

"Bon appetite!" I tell her and watch as she cuts a piece of chicken and places it in her mouth. Her eyes get wide as she chews and she starts nodding her head in appreciation.

"Wow, this is really good! I'm impressed," she says, as she takes a bite of asparagus.

"I'm happy you like it. Next time I'll make you my specialty, beef stroganoff."

She doesn't say anything about there not being a next time and I take that as a very good sign. We eat in compatible silence for a few minutes, watching each other relish in the taste of the delicious food.

"So, are we going to address the elephant in the room?" She asks, as she places her fork down, indicating she is done eating.

"I don't see any elephant in the room," I jokingly look around before stuffing my mouth with the last piece of chicken on my plate. I mentally kick myself for not making more food to consume in order to not have to talk yet about my past. I am just delaying the inevitable because if I want Layla in my life permanently, she needs to know everything.

She rolls her eyes at my sarcasm and gets right to the point. “Why do you think you killed your father?”

“I don’t think, I know I did,” I get up to take our plates away to put in the sink and she follows me.

“Chase, stop with the dishes and talk to me.” She shuts the faucet off that I had turned on to start washing the dishes, grabs my hand and pulls me toward the couch. We sit down and I can’t help but smile at her as she sits at the opposite end of the couch.

“There’s no way you intentionally killed your father. You would be in prison instead of sitting here with me.”

“My family is very wealthy, we could’ve paid the cops off.” This is not a far-fetched notion as my father made very sizable donations to the local police department.

“Alright Chase, since I invited you over for a serious conversation that you don’t seem to want to have, then you are free to leave as I’m tired and I have nothing more to say to you.” She stands up and is about to leave when I grab her hand and pull her back down to the couch, purposely closer to me.

“I’m sorry, you’re right. I apologize, but I need to hold your hand in order for me to talk seriously.” She gives me that sexy smirk that makes my groin tighten and appeases me by letting me hold her hand while we talk.

“My father was never one who was ever going to win the Father of the Year award, much less even be nominated.” I begin, taking a deep breath and exhaling out for this is going to be a long, hard story to tell. “I think he only agreed to have kids to pacify my mother and keep her quiet since he brought her from Germany to Canada where she had no family or friends. He met my mother at a party in Germany while backpacking across Europe. Once he found out that she was heir to a prestigious winery, he quickly charmed her, stayed in Germany to court her and got her to agree to marry him within a short amount of time.

I don't believe he was on vacation or that meeting her was a coincidence. I think he was in Europe on a mission to meet someone to change his life and identity."

"Why would he feel the need to change his identity?" She asks in confusion.

"When they got married, my father took on my mother's maiden name instead of her taking on his name. He led people to believe that it was a romantic gesture on his part since he claims to have been so in love with her, but I now know that it was all a facade to change his identity," I say with bitterness. "We didn't grow up knowing our paternal grandparents as he said they were dead, but we found out last year that was a lie." My father's death made international news and his parents contacted us, seeking money.

"Why would he lie about that?" Layla looks at me in confusion.

"Apparently, the apple didn't fall far from the tree as they were deadbeat parents. My father knew he was smart and good looking, so he left to form a new life. Once he married my mother, he made it known to her father that he wanted to help him with running Wilson Vineyards."

"For a while, my father's true colors did not come out. He worked hard and made a nice living for my mother and generated more revenue than my grandfather could have dreamed of. When my father suggested they open a winery in his homeland of Canada, my grandfather was on board with it. He purchased the land for the vineyard and my parents moved to Canada. I was born a year after their move and my brother came two years later."

"Unlike in the United States, ice wine is very popular in Canada, so it was a smart business decision on my father and grandfather's part to open a winery there. Profits were made within the first year and my father built a successful brand with the Wilson name. But as the years went on, he slowly pushed my grandfather out of the business in Canada. My father wanted complete control over the finances and decision-making. My grandfather wanted to make the company public and have a Board of Investors, but my father disagreed and wanted the company to stay private. So he re-paid my grandfather the money he paid for the land and took full control of running the Canadian winery. I always wondered why when my grandfather would come to visit he would ignore my father. Now I know."

"Is your grandfather still alive?"

"No, he died five years ago. My father made it a big public relations campaign about the death of the founder of Wilson Vineyards and how he loved his father-in-law for giving him the opportunity to run the company. When we went to Germany for the funeral and the reading of the Will, my father was livid to learn that he left all assets of the German winery to my aunt and cousins, who weren't involved in the family business, instead of him and my mother. My father filed to make Wilson Vineyards Canada a subdivision of his new company, Wilson Enterprises, with him as the sole owner so that my aunt and cousins couldn't have any control over what my father was doing. They hated my father and wanted nothing to do with him or have him involved in the business in Germany, so they had no problems with his actions."

"As the years went on, we saw my father less as he worked more. He would only show interest in being a father when he decided he needed to mold our future for us. He made it clear that I was going to be the heir of the family business since I am the oldest. My brother had shown interest in hockey and our father discovered that Rhys was a very talented hockey player, so his goal was to be in the NHL. My brother and I went along with the paths our father created for us because we actually wanted them as well. I was more interested in the branding and marketing side of Wilson Enterprises than the actual winery, much to my father's chagrin. But when he saw my ideas were making him money, he accepted where I wanted to be."

"So what went wrong? Sounds like everything was perfect."

"My father loved the attention he received from being the face of Wilson Enterprises. He wasn't happy with my growing popularity as the new face of the company, nor did he like it when people preferred me over him. Instead of being proud, he was jealous. So he started cutting me out of important decisions that I should have been part of, slashing my budgets and passing on me for promotions that I deserved. I started becoming suspicious, so I did some searching into the company's finances one day while working late. Things started to not make sense and one night, my father left his private laptop unlocked at work. My search through it found bank transfers of large amounts of money to an off shore account. He was embezzling money from the company."

Layla squeezes my hand as sympathy shines from her eyes.

"I went home to confront him, only to find him screwing his mistress. With the knowledge of the embezzlement and then seeing him betray my mother, I went crazy and beat the shit out of him. I left and went straight to a bar to get drunk. I woke up the following morning to my brother pouring water on my face, as I was so drunk the night before that I missed the phone call saying he died from a heart attack. I went straight home to comfort my mother, but she wanted nothing to do with me. My brother didn't speak to me. So, I left. Went to Seattle and just partied to numb the pain."

"Chase, you did not kill your dad," Layla whispers softly. "He was probably carrying around so much stress from his lies and deceit, that it was only a matter of time for that heart attack to occur."

I ignore her theory and continue. "His sudden death was all over the news, as was my absence. Two weeks after his funeral, my brother found me and asked me to come home. Telling me that creditors and banks were now calling, asking for payments of money they didn't seem to have. They needed me to come home to take charge and fix everything. I told him no, that he was in charge now. He got angry, we fought and he left. Next thing I knew there was a press release stating I was taking a sabbatical and my brother was now the interim CEO of Wilson Enterprises. That was over two years ago."

"How has the company been staying afloat for two years?"

"The wine was already made exported out for the season, so we made profits in that first year from the winery, but we sold off as many assets as we could with Wilson Enterprises and had to lay off a lot of people. This year's ice wine sales weren't so good. If we have another bad year, we will have to go under. For someone who knew nothing about the family business, Rhys has done an amazing job," I admit, secretly proud of my brother and what he has done to survive.

"Were you close with your brother?" She tilts her head while asking in curiosity.

"We were close once, but this has put a wedge between us. We are completely different people. Our temperaments are a mix of our parents, but looks wise, he looks like my mother and I look like our father. He blames me for ending his career in hockey. If I hadn't left, he would still be playing, possibly in the NHL."

"You don't know that, Chase."

"No, I do. He was really good. Scouts had been watching him from a young age." One of the few things my father would boast about was how good Rhys was at hockey and how numerous scouts were calling about him.

"What about your mother? Have you heard from her since?"

"Yes, she calls and texts me, begging me to come home. She says she loves me and that none of this is my fault, but I can't handle the pain I still hear in her voice. Luckily, she has been in Germany this past summer visiting family, so the phone calls have been at a minimum."

"How did you wind up becoming a paparazzi?" She quietly asks, her thumb rubbing circles inside my palm to soothe me.

"I was in Los Angeles for a weekend of debauchery with friends when I was confronted by a paparazzi who was Canadian. He started taking my picture, asking where I've been and I started chatting with him, asking him how he ended up where he was. My brother had been texting me, saying he was going to have to liquidate assets, asking me to help, but I was not ready to go home. So I figured I could help from afar by making money being a paparazzi. Photography was already a hobby of mine, so why not get paid to do something you love? Little did I know the seediness of the business. I started networking, making contacts who would accept bribes and I became good at it. The money started coming in and in some sick way, it made me feel like I was doing something to contribute to the mess back home, that I was making amends. But, it wasn't until I met you and Jenna and got to spend time with you both that made me realize that I am better than this business. The last thing I want to do is hurt innocent people."

She realizes I have reached the end of my story by my silence and takes a shaky breath. "Thank you for sharing your story with me. I know how hard that must have been for you and I hope you feel somewhat relieved, as it helps me understand you and why you did what you did in Las Vegas with revealing Jenna's secret." She untangles her fingers that were laced with mine and positions my hand so that she is holding it with both of hers. "I think you know that going home is the right decision. We can't pick our families and the damage that your father did is done. But you have the opportunity to save yourself, your brother and your mom and they are worth saving, as they are the two people who love you the most."

I nod my head because coming from her, everything sounds right.

"This is your chance to take ownership of your family business and take it to the level you always have dreamed of doing. Don't drown yourself in the facts of how the business became yours.

Relish in the fact that you can now make it your own and do good with it."

Her words are exactly what I need to hear. Her confidence in me gives me hope that if she can forgive me and move past my previous actions, then maybe my brother can too. She sat here with me, listened to my whole story without passing judgment, and is now trying to encourage me. Her affirmation in me makes me believe that I do need to try to change everything for the better with my family and Wilson Enterprises. As my eyes scan her face and see her sincerity, I realize this is exactly the woman I need by my side.

"Layla," I growl out, not being able to contain my need for her any longer. "I'm going to kiss you now." I don't give her time to protest as my lips are on her in seconds. I shove my hands into her hair and hold her face to mine, not giving her the opportunity to pull away from me. Any hesitation she had is gone as she kisses me back. I want to yell out in victory at finally having her willing to be in my arms.

Her lips part at the demands of my tongue and I moan at the taste of her sweetness. As we continue kissing, my hands grab her hips to pull her on top of me, needing her to straddle me so I can feel as close to her as I can get. She deepens our kiss by wrapping her arms around my neck and I can't stop my hands from roving down her back, over her delicious ass and to the side of her hips, pressing her down against me. My hands make their way back up and pull her shirt out from the waistband of her skirt. Her skin is scalding hot and I make my way up to her breasts, my fingers aching to play with her nipples. As soon as I start squeezing them, she gasps against my lips and starts to unconsciously move against my erection. My brain screams at me for the need to get inside of her. If I don't stop this now, I will soon explode against my pants. I reluctantly pull my hands away and break apart from our kiss. I rest my forehead against hers, our breaths mixing into one as we try to regain our composure.

"If we continue, I'm spending the night and never leaving," I breathe out, giving her the opportunity to make our decision. She leans back and stares at me, her lustful eyes searching mine as her breathing continues to even out. She releases my neck and her fingers slowly push my hair behind my ears. It is long enough now that it can curl right around the ear. I give her a grateful smile for getting it out of my face. She rubs her thumbs along my cheekbones as her eyes continue to stare into my soul. I see something change in them and when her hands let go of my face, I know I will not like her answer.

"I think it's late and time for you to head home."

I swallow my disappointment and nod my head in agreement. I want her to have zero doubts about being with me and as much as it physically pains me to leave right now, I will do so if she's not ready. I help her off my lap, my hands lingering on her skirt as I drag it back down her shapely thighs. Her eyes hover for a moment on the huge bulge in my pants before she turns around and heads toward the kitchen. I stand up and fix myself, trying to mentally think of anything else besides her to help ease my discomfort. She goes to the kitchen and brings us back glasses of water. She takes two big gulps of her drink, places it down on the counter and walks toward her door. I down the rest of my water before joining her. She opens the door and I stop right in front of her, needing to have one last look of her for my dreams tonight.

"Thank you for tonight. It meant a lot to me." I lean down and kiss her softly on the lips, inhaling her delicious coconut and vanilla sent one more time until tomorrow. I quickly pull away before it gets any deeper and make my way over the threshold of her door.

"Chase?" She calls out to me and I turn around, hoping she has changed her mind about me leaving. She is struggling with what she has to say, but her words soon stop me from approaching her.

"Don't fall in love with me, Chase," she swallows before continuing on, "I really don't want to hurt you."

My mind goes blank as her words are like tiny needles to my heart. I thought we made progress tonight, but I realize she has let the ghost of her dead husband come in to haunt her.

"Don't worry, Layla. You won't."

I turn on my heels and leave.

16

LAYLA

Chase's words from last night continue to occupy my thoughts this morning as I head to Jenna's offices to meet up with Robert. I tossed and turned all night long, my body still tingling from his touch, but my mind wide awake with wonder in his confidence that I won't unintentionally hurt him. Now that I know his past history, I see Chase in a different light. I understand his motives for what he did and I am relieved that he sees how harmful being a paparazzi can be. But what Chase wants from me is something I'm not ready to give yet, despite my feelings for him starting to change. His kisses completely rob me of my thoughts and the look in his eyes last night confirmed that he wants to consume me body and soul. I'm not ready to be consumed. I still need to focus on me and making more positive changes in my life.

And then there's the fact that he's going back to Vancouver.

I sigh in frustration, wishing that my entry into the dating world could be a little simpler. Why did I have to start becoming interested in someone who was leaving? I shake my head at myself when the ringing of my cell phone interrupts my thoughts and to my disappointment, I see that Robert is calling me instead of Chase.

"I'm on my way," I answer instead of saying hello so he would know that I'm close by.

"Great, but I need a favor. Can you make a detour and go to the pharmacy? I need condoms."

"What? I don't want to buy your condoms for you!" I exclaim, not understanding why this purchase can't happen later on by him.

"Please! I would buy your tampons for you! I don't have time today to go get some and I am fresh out with a hot date tonight," he explains while whining at the same time. His whining is like nails on a chalkboard and makes my ears hurt.

"The difference is that people would know that the tampons aren't for you, while people will assume the condoms are for me!" I say, already annoyed that he is asking me to go do this for him.

"So you're saying you now care about what people think of you?" He asks with sarcasm and I want to kick him in his balls so that he won't need condoms for a while. "First off, fuck them for judging. Secondly, they might praise you for practicing safe sex. Don't make a big deal of this. People, a.k.a women, buy condoms all the time."

I roll my eyes, knowing that he's right. "Fine, I will stop and get you condoms. Please tell me though this is the same guy you have been dating for the past two weeks."

"I am happy to report that it is," he says and I can hear him smiling into the phone.

"That is great, Robert!" I say enthusiastically, as I am genuinely happy for him.

"Oh, it won't last. How he eats his food is already driving me crazy," he laughs, and I can't help but shake my head at his pickiness.

"You're crazy," I laugh. "Okay, I'm about to go into the store. See you soon." I hang up and make my way to the aisle that contains the condoms. Of course, they would be on the bottom shelf and require me to bend down in my skirt in order for me to look at the package. I grab a box, but realize that Robert never told me what size to buy. I send him a quick text asking for size preference. While I wait for his response, I start to study each box, reading the differences in each brand.

"I recommend always buying the x-large size as you don't want to hurt the man's feelings."

The deep, masculine voice scares me and I drop the box of condoms as if it burned me. I bolt up and drop the other box on the floor. The man laughs and picks up both boxes off of the floor.

"I'm sorry if I scared you. You just had a confused look across your face while reading between each box so I thought I would help you." He is dressed in a three piece grey pinstripe suite with a white dress shirt and black tie. The suit shows off his thick, muscled body and hugs it in all the right places. His cologne smells expensive. His head is clean shaven, but his face is covered in dark hair that is closely trimmed to his strong jaw. His eyes are ice blue surrounded by dark thick lashes. He flashes a killer smile that shows off his bright white teeth. He uses his smile as a distraction, but I can't ignore my immediate assessment of him.

He radiates confidence.

He oozes sexuality.

He feels dangerous.

The old Layla would have taken one look at this man and made him her next one night stand. The new Layla is going to be polite and walk away, especially since another man has started to occupy her thoughts.

"Thank you," I stammer. "I'm buying these for a friend and he never told me what size to buy." As if on cue, my phone dings indicating I received a text message. I look down and sure enough, Robert's response is x-large. "Looks like you were right."

"What a beautiful messenger he has for himself." He doesn't even try to be discreet in checking out my body. I blush, his gaze making me uncomfortable. "He's very lucky to have a friend like you."

"Thanks again for your help," I say, wanting to get out of there as quickly as I can. I move past him and walk briskly to the cashier. I don't dare look back as my intuition is telling me that he's watching. I purchase the condoms swiftly and continue on my journey to meet up with Robert, willing myself to forget the encounter with the handsome stranger.

Two hours later with zero work done, I follow Robert out of his office and accompany him to his first meeting of the day. "Why am I coming to this meeting with you again?" I question, wondering if he even gave me a reason why my presence is required. As soon as I got there, we talked about the mystery man at the pharmacy and placed bets on whether Jenna says yes to Cal's proposal.

"Because the manager specifically asked for Jenna and since she is not here, I need you to impersonate her."

"I am not going to lie and say I am her! What if he already knows what she looks like? He will never hire you after knowing you lied to him and Jenna will be livid!"

"Okay fine, we won't say you are Jenna, but let's not reveal that you don't work for us unless he asks what your specific role is." Robert waves a taxi down and opens the door for me to get in.

"House of Royalty nightclub please," Robert tells the driver, and I gasp in recognition of the name.

"I just applied for a job there last week!" I say with excitement, hoping that I can ask the manager if he had a chance to look over my resume.

"You did?" Robert asks with a shocked expression on his face. "Since when have you been applying for new jobs?"

"Since the last trip to Los Angeles was a wake up call that I need to find a new job that has a healthier work environment for me."

"Honey, House of Royalty probably would not fit your new job requirement. I hear the basement is a swingers club!" He rubs his hands together in excitement.

"I don't think that's true." I hope it isn't, because if it is, I couldn't work there. Although, this job would keep me in the hospitality industry, it would be a new start with no travel. The position is for the assistant manager and with House of Royalty being one of the premiere nightclubs in Chicago, getting this position would make me more marketable for the future.

"I'm just hoping that the general manager is not as sexy as his name, otherwise I might cream my pants right in front of him." I look to see if the cab driver is paying attention to our conversation and sure enough, Robert gets a weird look directed at him from the rearview mirror.

"I hope this happens as well, as I would love to report that back to Jenna." I can just picture the shocked look on her face and an evil smile forms on my face.

"Oh please, I have already creamed my pants for Cal!" He waves his hand at his statement as if it's old news.

"Eew! That's disgusting, Robert! I really hope Jenna doesn't know about that." I shake my head at the mental image that Robert just provided.

He just shrugs his shoulders, as if it's no big deal to lust after his boss' boyfriend. "I'm a gay man and Cal is one fine mother fucker. Literally." He throws his head back and laughs at his own joke. I cover my eyes and groan, not comprehending how Jenna puts up with Robert sometimes. I need to change this subject fast, as I have no desire to learn what else Robert has fantasized about when it pertains to Cal.

"So what's the manger's name? I might ask if they've looked over my resume."

"I prefer you don't, as he might wonder why one of my

employees is looking for a job. Which by the way, I'll say you only work part-time for us if he asks." He gives me a direct look and I nod my head in acknowledgment of the plan. "His name is Torrin Richards. Isn't that the sexiest name you've ever heard?"

"Honestly, it sounds like a porn star name," I say, confused about what the fuss is for.

"Exactly!" Robert confirms and I can't help but laugh at his enthusiasm.

The cab pulls up to our destination and we get out. The club is a former historic mansion that is four stories, each story being a different theme. The building itself was built in the 1900s and looks majestic in its medieval setting with gargoyles sitting on the columns of the gated entrance.

After knocking on the door, we are ushered inside the building by a young lady who introduces herself as Crystal, one of the managers. She leads us to a conference room that is on the main level in the back of the building. She leaves us and I look around, admiring the wood paneling and leather decor of the room. The room is equipped with state of the art audio and visual equipment and seats twelve people around the oval wood table.

"This room is gorgeous. Remind me to ask him how much they would rent this room out as I know we would have clients interested in having a meeting here." I pull out a notebook and write Robert's request down. So engrossed am I in what I am doing that I fail to notice that the door has opened with the arrival of the general manger. Robert stands up to shake his hand and as I put my notebook down, I do a double take as I recognize the patent leather black loafers.

"Hi, I am Torrin Richards," the man from the pharmacy introduces himself, smiling at me like a Cheshire cat, as recognition lights up his eyes.

17

LAYLA

"THAT was creepy pharmacy dude?" Robert asks in doubt when I reveal who Torrin was once we are in the privacy of the taxi back to his office. Even though his smile indicated that he recognized me from this morning, Torrin remained completely professional and conducted business as if he had never met me before.

"Yes, that's him," I confirm, wondering if maybe I judged him to quickly from my encounter with him this morning.

"He can creep on me all day long if that's what you classify as creepy." Robert shakes his head, giving me a look as if I am crazy. "He's damn sexy!" I don't disagree with Robert, Torrin is indeed sexy.

Robert's phone vibrates and he looks down at it and then back at me with a smirk. "Layla, where's your phone?"

"In my bag, why?" I start rummaging through my tote bag so I can find my phone. He starts typing on his own and places it back inside the front pocket of his suit jacket.

"Your Canadian lover is stalking you." I finally locate my phone at the bottom of my purse to see I have five missed text messages and two missed calls from him, all sent within the last four hours.

Chase: Good morning, Angel! You probably didn't sleep well since you occupied my dreams all night long.

Chase: Was that too cheesy for you?

Chase: What are you doing tonight? I would like to take you out to dinner.

Chase: Angel, are you mad at me?

Chase: Layla, please call or text me back. I'm getting worried.

My phone being underneath my notebook and laptop must have prevented me from hearing or feeling its vibration. I immediately respond back.

Me: I'm so sorry! I've been with Robert at a meeting and my phone was buried in my purse. I have to work tonight.

Chase: Glad you are okay. What time and where? I'll meet you there.

I hesitate at answering him, trying to figure out what time I would be done meeting with the manager and bartender.

Me: Meet me at eight p.m. There is a really good sushi restaurant around the corner that we can go to.

I quickly look up the address of the bar and include it in my response.

Chase: Looking forward to seeing you, Angel.

"Are you done sexting yet?" Robert asks, while trying to look over my shoulder at my texts.

"None of your business." I click off my phone and put it back in my purse. Robert looks at me with a raised eyebrow, waiting for my response. "No, we weren't sexting. We haven't even had sex. We were confirming plans for dinner tonight."

He gives me a mischievous grin and proceeds to pull out the box of condoms from his work bag. "Here, let's split these. I have a feeling you will need them. Zero doubts that Chase probably wears an x-large." He opens the box and pours half the condoms in my bag.

"Sorry, I can't recall." The lie runs smoothly from my lips as I completely recall seeing his erection bulging from his pants last night and noted his rather large size.

"You'll be able to recall tonight after it's in your mouth." Robert throws his head back in laughter at my shocked expression. "Oh c'mon, Layla! It's bound to happen sooner rather than later with the amount of time you've been spending with him."

"We're just friends, Robert," I say, while I look out the window, not wanting to meet his gaze.

"Bullshit, Layla. There's more to it and you just don't want to admit it."

His tone of voice makes me look at him. "He's going back to Vancouver soon." I counter back.

"Give him a reason to come back, Layla. If you did, he will be back in a heartbeat," he says with a serious expression.

"I don't think it's a good idea to get involved with anyone until I work more on myself."

"While I agree that you need to continue your journey of self-improvement, you of all people should know that life is short and can be gone in a second. Don't wait for happiness, Layla, when it might be within your grasp just because you want to make yourself better. You will never be perfect. No one will ever be perfect."

I let my gaze linger on his before turning back to the window, his words resonating with me as we sit in silence. While Robert is right and life is precious and short, I still would like to check off some items on my self-help list before getting into a new relationship.

The taxi pulls up in front of Robert's office. He gets out and turns around to help me. "Are you coming?" He asks when he notices I haven't moved.

"No, I have my weekly meeting with my boss in thirty minutes so I should just head to the office." I give the taxi driver my office address to program into his navigation.

"Ok, call me tomorrow, and I hope you have some sex tonight!" He shuts the door and waves at me through the window with a wicked smile on his face.

The rest of my work day moves quickly and before I know it, it is eight p.m. Once work is finished, I decide to wait for Chase in the booth the head bartender and I occupied while conducting our meeting. I slowly nurse the vodka tonic that he had waiting for me when I arrived. I never realized how much I was drinking on the job before now and am quite amazed at what a functioning alcoholic I had become. Not that it is something to be proud of. I decide to take a small sip, hoping that the melted ice has since watered it down while I wait for Chase. My eyes roam over the main area of the bar, noting how much more crowded it has gotten since I've arrived because of people coming to take advantage of Friday night happy hour. The booth I'm in is elevated higher than the main floor, but people have congregated by the entrance, making it hard for me to see who is coming in and out. A young group of girls standing by the door start whispering to each other and nodding their heads at whomever just walked in. Feeling confident that it's Chase, I decide to stand up and see if I can get a better view of him to catch his attention. But instead of it being Chase, my eyes widen in shock as I attract the attention of the cool ice blue eyes of Torrin Richards.

How the hell have I never met this man before, but in one day I see him three times?

I immediately sit back down and scramble to get my phone to ask Chase where he is when I see that I already have a text message from him.

Chase: Angel, I'm sorry, I'm still stuck on a conference call

with my brother. Come to my house and I'll cook for you once this call is done. I promise to keep my hands to myself...for at least the first hour.

I groan out loud, wishing we had planned this ahead of time. I start to text him back, asking for his address when I feel the seat underneath me dip. I look up to see Torrin has taken it upon himself to sit next to me in my booth.

"How is it that I have grown up in this city and have never seen you before, but in one day, I get the pleasure of seeing you three times?" He asks the same question I had just been thinking.

"That's really creepy as I was thinking the same thing," I smile politely at him while trying to put some distance between us.

"I think it's a sign." His smile catches my attention, his white teeth almost hypnotic. His lips are the perfect shade of pink and look firm and inviting. I quickly glance up at him, only to see that he saw me watching his lips. I can't help but shiver from the glint that enters his eyes.

"I don't believe in signs," I say and immediately gulp down the rest of my vodka tonic to calm my nerves.

Why does this man make me feel nervous?

He raises his hand and catches the attention of the bartender to bring us two more drinks. "Well, I believe in signs and I think I know exactly what fate has in store for you and I."

18

CHASE

I was feeling like an asshole when I texted Layla saying I was going to be late due to my conference call with my brother and our marketing director.

When fifteen minutes passed by after I sent her a text and I heard nothing, I didn't think much of it as maybe she was still working.

When thirty minutes passed by and she still had not answered my second text, I was worried.

And when the forty-five minute mark came and went without a word from her, I was frantic.

So imagine how livid I am when I walk into the bar an hour later to see her having a good time with another man.

I am seeing fucking red!

In order to calm down before confronting her, I order a glass of water and sit at the opposite end of the bar to observe them. The guy has his arm thrown across the back of the booth where she sits, his eyes trained on her chest as he says something to her that makes her laugh. Her laughter is loud and boisterous - not her normal laughter when she's in control. I see an empty shot glass and a tall regular glass that has clear liquid with a lime in it that I bet is not water. When she looks in my direction and doesn't acknowledge my existence, I know Layla is drunk.

And so does he.

He is probably the reason why she got drunk.

I study him and can see why women might think he is good looking. He looks like he could be an MMA fighter dressed up in a suit. He wears his suit tight which makes him look powerful. Some women find power sexy.

I see him as anything but powerful.

I see him as a dangerous predator.

And he has his sights set on Layla.

I down the rest of my water and move slowly to their table. So engrossed are they in each other that they don't even notice when I stand in front of their table.

"Layla," I command in a strong voice, wanting to make sure she sees me this time. She looks in my direction and her eyes are watery and glazed in that incoherent alcoholic state.

"CHASE!" She yells so loudly that the man sitting next to her backs away from her. "You are finally here!"

My anger lessons at her happiness upon my arrival. "Yes, I'm here because I was getting concerned when you didn't text me back after I asked you to meet me at my house."

Her face scrunches up in confusion and she looks back and forth between me and the guy next to her. She looks around for her purse, finds that it's right next to her on the side not being taken over by douchebag and rummages through it until she finds it. She squints at the screen and then snorts out a chuckle.

"I wrote it, but forgot to hit the send button!" She starts to laugh hysterically and then slaps douchebag on the shoulder. "It's all your fault as you were distracting me."

"I am very good at being a distraction," he says in a flirtatious tone that makes me want to punch him.

"Oh, I bet you are!" Layla continues laughing hysterically and turns her attention back to me. "Chase, you are not going to believe this. I met him in the convenience store this morning while buying condoms for Robert. Then Robert asked me to accompany him to his first meeting and guess who it was with?" She points to douchebag with an awed expression on her face. "This guy! And then, I was waiting here for you and he shows up instead! How much of a coincidence is all of that?" Her head sways down, the alcohol taking over her reflexes to hold her head up.

"Interesting coincidence. What did you say your name was?" I narrow my eyes at the hard look on his face. He removes his arm from the back of her seat and pushes himself out of the booth.

"I didn't say." He looks at me with disdain and then immediately hides it when turning his attention to Layla. "Thank you for letting me keep you occupied while your date was an hour late. I look forward to seeing you on Monday to go over the job opening." He sizes me up before nodding his head at me and leaves.

As soon as Layla is more coherent, I'll be grilling her on this asshole. Maybe I can talk to Cal to have his fancy private investigators get full details on him. I turn my attention back to Layla just in time as she sways while standing up from the booth. I wrap my arm around her waist to hold her up and carry her tote bag with my other arm. We walk outside and get into an awaiting taxi. Fortunately, with it being a Friday night, there are plenty lined up outside the bar. I give him my address and as soon as I'm done talking, Layla grabs my face and starts kissing me.

"Layla," I groan, as she starts to trail kisses down my neck. Her hand is on my pants, fumbling with the button to my jeans. She manages to unbutton it before I move her hand away. "Not here, Layla. Let's wait until we get to my place."

"Don't tell me you don't want this," she seductively says, continuing to move my zipper down and slip her hand inside my pants. To distract me, she brings her lips back up to mine and sears me with a hot, wet kiss. Her breath tastes like the signature cinnamon whiskey she enjoys and my control starts to slip. Her tongue slips through my lips and I moan as her hand touches my erection. She continues her assault on my lips and my dick, the outside world slowly starting to fade. She gently bites down on my lower lip, squeezing my shaft at the same time and I almost cum right there in her hand. Her lips leave mine and I watch in a daze as her head goes down to finish me off. My cock starts twitching at the thought of being inside her hot, wet, mouth but before she can latch on, I place my hands on her shoulders and pull her up.

"Layla, not here!" I demand and the tone of my voice not only gets her attention, but that of the taxi driver as he looks at me in his rearview mirror.

"Wow, since when did you become such a fuddy duddy?" She slurs, disappointment written all over her face.

I close my eyes and count to ten, praying that I can keep my control in check. We only have a couple more blocks to go until we arrive at my apartment. If making her mad keeps her hands - and mouth - off me, then so be it.

"The taxi driver might become distracted by hearing that succulent mouth of yours. I wouldn't want us to crash, Angel." I lean in close to her and whisper in her ear. "Just another five minutes and then you can have your wicked way with me in the privacy of my place." I wink at her and this seems to placate her for the time being. What seems like the hardest five minutes of my life from refraining to touch her, we finally arrive at my apartment. I pay the driver and help Layla out and up to my apartment.

As soon as we get inside, I deposit her on the couch and go to the kitchen to get her a glass of water. "Did you eat dinner?" I question, feeling guilty that I let her down by not showing up on time.

"Nope!" Her emphasis on the word makes me smile. No wonder she is drunk with the amount of alcohol she has imbibed on an empty stomach. I walk back to the couch with her water.

"How about I make you a sandwich? I'm sure you're hungry."

"I am not hungry for food," she says and proceeds to try to stand up, but dizziness from the alcohol causes her to sit back down.

"Why don't you watch some television while I make you a snack?" I don't give her a chance to answer as I head back to the kitchen and prepare her some eggs and toast. I see her flick through the channels and settle on a movie. Eight minutes later, I carry a tray with our food out to her but stop short at the sight of her.

She is slumped over, snoring in her sleep.

19

LAYLA

The first thing I feel when I start to regain consciousness is the slow, pounding hammer in my head. I try to open my mouth, but it feels as dry as a desert. My eye lids feel like they are weighed down with sand bags and refuse to open. I groan out in frustration as my limbs are heavy and unresponsive when I try to move.

"Good morning, gorgeous," Chase says way too loudly for my ringing head. I am one hundred percent confident that gorgeous is the last thing I look right now. I manage to open my eyes and see him sitting beside me on the couch. His beautiful chest is bare, his carved out pectorals and beautiful hard six pack abs on full display. His pajama pants hang low on his hips, showing off his sculpted V-shaped torso that disappears into his pants. My eyes scan his body up and down, my tongue immediately feeling thick as the desire to lick every inch of him grows. I snap out of my thoughts and look underneath the blanket at myself to see that I am still fully clothed. I must have passed out on the couch and he covered me up with a blanket to sleep. My heart warms a little at the fact that he could have easily taken advantage of my inebriated state, but instead was a perfect gentleman.

"Hi yourself," I croak out, my throat feeling as if I swallowed a hundred nails. He hands me a glass of water and I give him a grateful smile. I take a deep swallow, the cold water putting out the flames inside my mouth.

"Are you hungry?" He asks and my stomach answers him in a growl. He laughs in his low, seductive way and stands up to head to the kitchen. "I will make us some breakfast. Make yourself at home and relax." I lay back down and try to close my eyes, but visions of Chase's half naked body keep appearing, making me feel very uncomfortable. I reopen my eyes and look around his apartment instead as a distraction from my inappropriate thoughts. It is a small studio apartment where there are no walls separating the kitchen from the living room to the bedroom. Decor is minimal, reminding me that his time here is short.

"Did you have to sign a long term lease for this place?" I ask, curious if he would need to stay longer than the two weeks he says he has left here in order to not break a lease.

"I'm on a month-to-month lease," he says as he scoops eggs out of the pan and onto the plates. "Breakfast is almost ready."

I get up and use the restroom before sitting down to eat. I look at myself in the mirror with disgust, confirming that I look exactly like the hot mess I feel I am. I wash the mascara off from underneath my eyes and slather some toothpaste onto my finger to attempt to brush my teeth. I rinse out my mouth and go out to join him. I sit down on one of his barstools and as he hands me my plate of food, he deliberately brushes my hands with his after I take it from him. The warmth of his touch makes me shiver. There is nothing sexier than a man taking care of a lady, but he shouldn't have had to take care of me last night. I shouldn't have drunk as much as I did. I look down in embarrassment, grateful that he was there and that he still continues to take care of me this morning. I look up at him and he smiles, his desire for me still prevalent in his eyes, despite seeing me at a low point last night. Memories of my actions in the cab ride start to become less hazy and I become completely horrified at my behavior.

"What is wrong? Your face is all red," he asks with concern. I take a sip of water, hoping it will help cool down my blush.

"I'm sorry about last night," I look down at my food, not wanting him to see the shame in my eyes. "Thank you for taking care of me."

"I was happy I was there to take care of you, but I'm the one who owes you an apology as I left you alone for an hour." While that is true, if it was for the sake of dealing with business with his brother, I can't get mad at that.

"It was fine. Was everything okay with your brother?"

"Yes, everything is fine." He puts down his fork and I notice that he has already inhaled his eggs and toast. He wipes his mouth with a napkin and memories of his hard, hot lips on mine start to burn up my cheeks again. "But, I don't want to talk about my brother. I do want to talk about that guy you were with last night. Who was he?"

I blink my eyes, trying to focus my thoughts on his question instead of his lips. "That was Torrin Richards, the general manager of the House of Royalty nightclub. I met him with Robert earlier in the day."

"And you're meeting with him on Monday about a job?" He quizzes me with narrowed eyes.

"I told you that?" I ask in surprise, trying to recall last night's conversation.

"No, he mentioned it when he was saying goodbye to you." He sits back and crosses his arms over his chest. The movement makes my eyes go immediately to his pink, hard nipples.

"Oh…" I shake my head, willing myself to look at his face and not at his chest. "Well, yes, I have a meeting with him to discuss the opening they have at the club."

He tilts his head with a questioning look. "Do you really think that is a good idea?"

"Why wouldn't it be? I have hit the ceiling with my current job and the traveling is getting tiresome. His job opening is for someone to run the special events that his club hosts. This is the stepping stone I need in order to qualify for future job opportunities at the elite venues in Chicago."

"I'm confident that you are overqualified for this position. I think you should continue looking elsewhere." He stands up and dumps his plate in the kitchen sink, pours himself and me a cup of coffee and comes back to sit down with me while I finish eating.

"I'm still continuing to look elsewhere, but there is no reason for me not to meet with him on Monday. It's just an interview, there's no harm in that." I take another bite of my food, intrigued by what his reasoning may be.

"There is something about him, Layla, that I don't like. I want you to stay away from him." I almost choke on my food, not prepared for him to demand me to stay away. *Who does he think he is to tell me what to do?*

"Excuse me? You have no right to tell me what to do, Chase!" I say in anger when suddenly realization hits me. "Wait a minute, are you jealous?" The concept seems so foreign to me as Chase has nothing to be jealous about when it pertains to Torrin.

"He is dangerous, Layla. Stay away from him." He commands as he picks up my plate and takes it into the kitchen for me.

"Who says he is dangerous, Chase? Have you investigated him yet?" I can't hide the hint of disgust that filters into my voice over the lengths that Chase goes through to find out information on someone when he is a paparazzi.

"Not yet, but I will and I look forward to telling you I told you so." His tone gets playful and he winks at me. I can't help but roll my eyes at him, secretly hoping he finds nothing bad on Torrin.

"I'm done with this conversation. It's time for me to go." I stand up and head toward the couch to grab my purse.

"Why? What do you have planned for today?" He stands in front of me, blocking my path towards the door. He invades my personal space by standing so close to me that my breasts are touching his bare chest. Despite the layers of clothes I have on, I feel the sexual energy radiating off of him and my nipples immediately stand to attention.

"I need to report in the two client meetings from yesterday so I am not behind on Monday with work." I stare at his neck, refusing to look down at our bodies touching or his eyes that would suck me right into staying longer with him.

"Let's go see a movie tonight." He cups my chin and forces it up, giving me no choice but to look at him. It has been a very long time since I have been to the movies and the thought of going actually sounds fun. Plus, it would be two hours of me not having to talk or look at him, which would keep me clear headed.

"Okay," I confirm with no hesitation. His eyes light up with delight and he quickly plants a swift, hard kiss on my lips.

"Excellent! Let me get a shirt and I will walk you downstairs to get a taxi." He turns around and as I watch his delectable, hard, bubble shaped ass strut to his dresser, I start to think maybe going to the movies with him tonight is not such a good idea.

20

CHASE

I tap my foot against the concrete as I anxiously await Layla outside the movie theater. I was ecstatic when she agreed to go to the movies with me as it finally gives me a chance to take her out on a date. Going to the movies is not my preferred destination for a first date, but with Layla still having reservations about me, I will take whatever I can get from her.

I look up and down the street for her when my eyes suddenly focus on her approaching figure. She is wearing a long floral dark blue dress with a dark denim jean jacket to protect her from the chill that is in the autumn air. Her silky hair is styled half up, half down and she has minimal make up on with just mascara and pink lip gloss. I exhale a shaky breath as my heart is racing at how stunning she is. I watch as her eyes scan my body and I quietly groan at the sexy smirk she gives me as she stops right in front of me.

"Hello, Angel. You look stunning." I kiss her forehead and close my eyes as I inhale her scent that is now permeated in my brain. I take the smallest step back from her, needing to control myself as all I want to do is grab her hand, run back to my house and make love to her all night long.

"You look amazing yourself. I love your jacket." She lifts her hand to feel the leather of my jacket. Heat goes straight to my penis and I wince at its tightening.

"Let's go inside and find some seats." I pre-purchased the tickets based on what Layla told me she wanted to see. Once inside, we stop first at the concession stand to get some popcorn, candy and drinks. As we enter our designated theater and decide where to sit, I notice that our theater is mostly empty, majority of the population seeing the new action superhero movie that just came out instead of the drama movie we are seeing. We sit down and I lift up the arm rest that is between us in order to be closer to her and to comfortably share the popcorn. I hold the popcorn in my lap and we start to eat while enjoying the previews. Her laughter at one of the previews draws my attention to her and I watch as she reaches into the tub of popcorn, grabs a handful and slowly starts to eat. I am mesmerized as I watch her tongue dart out to stick to a piece of popcorn before pulling it inside her mouth. She reaches into the bag of cotton candy that is on her lap and as her tongue darts out again to take a bite, visions of that hot tongue licking the tip of my cock start to invade my thoughts. I start to shift uncomfortably in my seat, grateful that the popcorn is hiding my growing erection.

The previews end and the movie starts to play. She stops eating to focus her full attention on the movie. I grab her candy off her lap, place it inside the tub with the rest of the popcorn and put it under my seat. I take off my jacket and place it in on her lap as I saw her shiver earlier. The movie theater might be cold, but my blood is boiling from the desire I have for her. She gives me a grateful smile and my eyes can't help but zero in on that mouth of hers. Images of her tongue won't stop and my brain, in conjunction with my body, has decided that my focus should be on her and not this movie.

I look down to see how accessible her skirt is and discover that it is peaking out of the sides of my jacket that is on her lap. Her legs are crossed with her right leg over her left, giving me access to my preferred destination. I sneak my hand down and proceed to bring the fabric up in order for my hand to get inside. I slowly drag my fingers toward her core, refusing to touch her skin until I am hovering right over her mound. As soon as I know I am there, my fingers land on top of her panties. She jumps up in surprise, which causes her legs to uncross. I deliberately keep my head straight and pretend to watch the movie as I sneak my fingers lower.

"Chase, what are you doing?" She whispers as I start to rub her clit against the fabric of her underwear. They feel satiny and I am dying to see what they look like on the floor next to my bed. I move my finger lower and I feel the hot flesh of her folds leading towards her ass, indicating that she is wearing a thong. I swallow loudly, the images of her sweet, round ass in a thong almost doing me in. I notice out of the corner of my eye that she is looking at me, but has not told me to stop. She looks around to see if anyone is watching us. We have the aisle all to ourselves and the only other people in the theater with us are more than three rows ahead. I keep looking straight, pretending I am engaged in watching the movie when really I am holding my breath to see if she is going to let me continue. I get my answer when she sinks lower in her seat and spreads her legs further apart. I also sink lower, my eyes trained on the movie as my fingers continue their assault on her. I can feel her start to become distracted by my touch as she leans her neck against the back of the seat and her hips start thrusting up. Her slow thrusts cause my fingers to sink lower and I swipe her thong aside to slip a finger inside of her. I hiss in my breath, imagining that it is my dick and not my finger being incased inside her silky wetness. I push my finger in farther and when I feel her walls tighten against it, my cock starts to pulsate against my pants, demanding that it be inside her. I open my mouth to help my breathing and glance at her. Her eyes are hooded with desire and she looks at me with longing as I pull my finger out of her warmth to massage her clit. When she moans and bites her lip to silence her noises, I reach forward for her neck with my left arm, which forces me to turn my body more towards her, giving my hand easier access as I turn it around to cup her more. I pull her mouth to mine and plunge my tongue into her, silencing her whimpers of desire. The touch of our tongues against each other causes us to moan loudly and I peak my eyes open to see if anyone is watching. When I only see the back of everyone's heads, I increase the pace of my fingers as I press harder while rubbing her up and down. She starts to pant against my mouth, her body moving faster against my finger. Our tongues start their own wild dance and as soon as I feel her begin to tense, I unlock our mouths and shove her face into my chest to muffle the screams of her release. I ease my grip on her neck as I feel her body's spasm slowly start to fade. She keeps her face pressed into my chest as our breathing starts to even out.

As minutes start to pass by and she doesn't move, I start to think she has fallen asleep. Her face is facing the screen, so I can't tell if her eyes are open or closed. I sink lower in my seat so her head can rest comfortably against my chest and I start to focus on what is happening in the movie. *What the hell is going on?* I wonder as I feel the restraints against my erection loosen and realize that Layla has just unbuttoned my pants and pulled down my zipper. Her hand on my cock paralyzes my tongue from telling her to stop and before I can predict her next move, her head moves forward and her hot, little mouth is on me. The feeling of being inside her mouth completely takes my breath away. Any dreams of what I thought getting a blow job from Layla might feel like do not even come close to reality as reality is fucking heaven. A tiny voice inside my head tells me I need to make her stop since anyone can walk up and down the aisle and see what she is doing. Instead I ignore that voice when she grips me with both hands and slowly takes me in as far as she can.

Holy fucking shit!

My hands start caressing her head as she starts to lick up and down my hard shaft, one of her hands tightening around it, while her other hand slips underneath my balls and starts squeezing. I push back her hair, needing to watch her as she takes me in. She looks at me out of the corner of her eyes and I moan even louder at the look of pure seduction on her face.

"Angel..." I groan, as I feel myself hitting the back of her throat. I won't be able to handle this much longer as I was already worked up from pleasuring her. "I'm about to cum," I warn, giving her enough time to get off of me. Instead, she grips harder and sucks faster. My hips start to buck wildly at her increasing speed. I quickly pull the jacket off her lap and shove my face in it to hide my yells of pleasure as I release into her mouth.

Once my body stops shuddering, I remove the jacket from my face and stare up at the ceiling as I try to catch my breath. I turn my head to look at her and she is sitting there calmly, her drink in her hand, as she stares straight ahead at the movie.

Did I just dream this?

She brings the straw to her mouth to suck the contents of her drink and her mouth wrapped around my dick suddenly flashes in my head.

Best first date ever!

Two hours later, we walk out of the movies like embarrassed teenagers. I grab her hand and walk her further down the sidewalk. She can barely look at me and when she does, she can't control the blush that keeps staining her cheeks. She is glowing and I want to make her look and feel like this every day of the week. I am about to ask her if she wants to come home with me when we both feel our phones vibrate at the same time, alerting us to a text message. We pull out our phones to see we have received a text message from Cal.

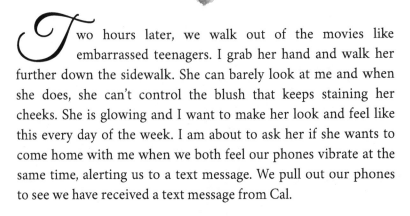

Cal: Family dinner tomorrow at six p.m., our house. Much to discuss. See you then.

"I wonder what that is all about?" I notice that Robert is also included in the text and I look at Layla in confusion. She stares a little bit longer at her phone before meeting my gaze.

"No clue. I guess we'll see tomorrow." Her smile doesn't reach her eyes and I see our moment of closeness is gone. I don't understand why Cal's text message would trigger her, but it did.

"Do you want to get a bite to eat?" I ask, hoping she says yes, but my intuition telling me she will say no.

She quickly looks up at me, but doesn't hold my gaze long as she looks toward the street. "I'm actually not that hungry. I think we should call it a night."

I grab her hands to gain her attention back. "Why don't we call it at night at my place? I promise to behave and only snuggle with you." I place my hands on her cheeks, my eyes memorizing her luscious lips. She contemplates for a moment, the struggle evident in her stormy blue eyes.

"Maybe another night? I'm actually quite tired from the most memorable movie I have ever seen." I throw my head back and laugh, feeling slightly better that she feels the same way I do as I will never, *ever* forget what transpired in that theater between us tonight.

"Okay, Angel, another night then. Let's get you a taxi." I hail a cab for her and open the door for her to get in. But before she gets in, I kiss her soundly on the mouth, hoping she has vivid dreams of what is more to come between us.

"Sweet dreams, Angel." I shut the door and watch the taxi speed away until the taillights disappear from my view.

21

LAYLA

I wake up this morning feeling like a walking tornado with the way my emotions are swirling everywhere. I am proud of myself for the positive changes I have been trying to instill as a normal routine, including a more positive outlook on my life. But right now, my mood is as dark as the storm clouds that are covering the city and I can't pinpoint one main reason why. My demons are battling hard today, whispering that I should stay home and hide with a bottle of Tito's. If it wasn't raining, I would go for a walk. Instead, I stay cooped up in my apartment, memories teasing me of my previous life. My grief counselor has taught me that I need to face these emotions head on and write down what I am feeling. So, I sit down and write out every emotion I am feeling to try to associate a subject with it.

Anxiety - Everyone leaving me.

Sadness - Being alone for the rest of my life.

Dread - Every day I come home to an empty apartment filled with memories of Charlie.

Scared - My evolving feelings for Chase.

I stare at the last line as if it slapped me in the face. I just need to have some tough love with myself for a change about how I really feel about Chase. The old Layla would have chewed him up and spit him out already without even looking back. This new Layla feels like she is back in high school discovering her first crush. The man has started to consume my every thought to the point of distraction. I look forward to his text messages every morning. I look forward to hearing his voice when he calls. His perception of me matters. And the way my body physically reacts to him every time I am near him makes me believe that he is secretly a hypnotist.

I haven't felt this way since Charlie, and while I should be ecstatic that I finally found someone to have these feelings for, instead I want to hide in my room and never let anyone in.

Because being alone is easier.

Being alone makes me feel safe.

Being alone won't leave me with a broken heart.

Being alone guarantees that no one I love will be taken away from me.

I roll my eyes at myself, knowing that my thinking is dangerous and would have everyone who loves me extremely worried. But if I am going to be truly honest, then I also need to admit that deep down I don't want to be alone. I miss sharing my life with someone. I want to have kids someday. But do I want to take that chance on someone like Chase?

My father always told me that the best way to face a major decision in life is to write out the pros and cons. I turn my piece of paper over and start to write out the pros and cons of Chase Wilson:

Pros

Smart

Funny

Sweet

Amazing kisser

Attentive

Driven
Resourceful
Independent
Sexy

Cons
Deceived me in the past
Returning to Vancouver
Former playboy
Smooth talker
Family drama
Crumbling business
Paparazzi
Way too sexy

I go over each and every word in my head multiple times, waiting for the 'a-ha' moment on how to proceed forward with Chase when my phone dings with a text message.

Chase: Good morning, Angel. I trust you slept well and had numerous wet dreams involving me as I did you. I am looking forward to seeing you later.

No, I didn't sleep well last night as I tossed and turned all night long from the cravings he erupted from my body for him. And, when I did finally fall asleep, he intruded on my dreams.

I crumple up the paper in my fist, throw it in the trash and decide to do two of the things I do best - delay making a decision regarding Chase and go shopping.

Six hours of retail therapy and the only thing I walk away with is a basket of goodies for Avery. I decided to buy her some of her favorites toys, some snacks and clothes. I worked hard making the basket look pretty and as I ride the elevator up to Jenna's apartment, I am excited to watch her open it. I knock on the door and to my surprise, Chase answers looking devilishly sexy in a black, long sleeve V-neck sweater, jeans and high top dress shoes. *Traitor,* I silently scream at my heart as it starts to beat faster at the sight of him.

"Hello, Angel," he whispers seductively and swiftly kisses me on the lips. "I've missed you today." I can't help but smile at him, but my smile soon fades when he turns around and I see Jenna watching us with raised eyebrows.

Busted!

"Auntie Layla!" Avery screams, as she runs past both Chase and Jenna toward me, and crashes into my legs.

"Avery Doodle, I have missed you so much!" I squat down to her level and squeeze her in the tightest hug her little body can withstand. "I brought you some presents. Were you the best girl on your trip with mommy and daddy?"

"Yes, Auntie Layla!" She nods her head in excitement, her eyes wide as she looks in anticipation at the basket I am holding.

"Good girl. Go take this into the living room to open." As soon as I hand her the basket, she takes off running down the hall, nearly knocking Jenna down as she passes her to the living room.

"Mommy, look what Auntie Layla got me!" She yells as she sets the basket down on the coffee table and starts rummaging through it to look at all of her presents.

"I see," Jenna says as she watches her daughter. "Aunt Layla spoils you rotten."

I stand back up and walk toward Jenna to give her a hug. As I pull back, I study her face and see a drastic difference in her from five days ago. Her gaunt, pale look is gone, the bags under her eyes have vanished and there is an amused twinkle in her eyes as she watches me look her over. She is glowing with happiness, which makes me wonder if we have a future wedding to celebrate.

"I've missed you, Jens," I say with sincerity. I squeeze her hands and feel no engagement ring on her finger. Either Cal decided to wait to ask her or she said no like I predicted.

"I've missed you too. Seems like we have a lot to catch up on," she winks at me and quickly nods her head over at Chase, who is standing by the dining room table talking to Robert. "Can you meet me for our morning workout tomorrow?"

"Yes, but we are going to have to make it short because I've got to get home to shower and change for a job interview I have."

Her eyes go wide with excitement as she has been wanting me to look for a new job for years now. "Wow, we really do have a lot to talk about." We walk toward the couch together to watch Avery open her gifts.

I see Cal come out of Jenna's office and I go over to give him a hug. "You were right," he whispers in my ear, answering my curiosity about whether he proposed or not. While I usually relish in the fact of predicting when I am right, this instance is not one of them.

"Don't give up," I whisper back to him, hoping he isn't discouraged by her refusal at his proposal.

"Never!" He says seriously before giving me a wink. He turns his attention to Avery and sits down on the ground beside her to look over her presents. "Avery, what has Aunt Layla brought you?"

She shows off her new toys and clothes, but I can't help but see disappointment on her beautiful, little face as she keeps looking into the basket even after it is empty.

"Avery, what's wrong? Didn't you like your presents?" I ask, as Chase and Robert join us at the couch to watch her.

"I do like my presents, Auntie Layla, but I was really hoping you were going to get me some cum juice to try." Silence permeates the air as we all try to comprehend in shock what she just said. I look over at Jenna, whose eyes seem to be bulging out of her sockets. Robert is covering his mouth with his hand and looks away, so Avery does not see him laughing. Chase has a questioning smile on his face, as if he doesn't think he heard her correctly. And Cal stares at his child in confusion, before tilting his head and looking at Jenna.

"Did our daughter just say what I think she just said?"

"Daddy, Auntie Layla said cum juice is your favorite kind of juice and I think it's unfair that I haven't tried it yet since things that are your favorite are my favorite too," Avery says in her sweet, innocent five-year-old voice. Cal gives me a quizzical look while Robert can't hide his laughter anymore. My eyes shoot daggers at him while he laughs at my expense.

"What interesting things you have learned this summer, Avery," Cal says smoothly as he looks at Jenna, who is covering her face with her hands in embarrassment.

"Wait until you hear what she has learned from Robert," I snidely remark, which shuts up the cackling that is coming from him. He gives me the evil eye and mouthes 'fuck you' at me. I smile and blow a kiss at him with my middle finger.

"So, can I have some?" Avery asks again, batting her eyelashes at Cal to try to get what she wants.

"While your Aunt Layla is correct that it is my favorite kind of juice," Cal look towards Jenna and winks, "it is not appropriate for children and is only for adult consumption." He explains with a slow, devilish smile.

"It's time for dinner!" Jenna screeches in a high voice as she jumps up from the couch and starts heading to the kitchen. "Avery, please put your new toys away and help Mommy set the table."

"But Mommy..." Avery whines before continuing on her relentless attempt at getting her way.

"NOW!" Jenna commands and Avery gets up from the floor,

puts all her new presents inside the basket and takes it to her room.

"I can't wait to hear this story!" Chase says, as we enter the kitchen to pile our plates with the Italian food that Jenna had brought in. We all get our plates of food and sit down at the table to eat. For the next hour, we talk about Cal and Jenna's trip, laugh at the cute things Avery says and enjoy each other's company.

"Avery, why don't you get ready for bed and then you can watch TV for a little bit in Mommy and Daddy's room?" Cal suggests after we have finished dessert. Avery reluctantly goes to her room with Jenna to get ready for bed. Once she's ready and kisses us all good night, Jenna takes Avery into her room to turn on the TV and then comes back to the table and sits down next to Cal.

"Alright everyone, let's talk some business since we don't have little ears with us anymore. Thank you for joining us tonight on such short notice. Jenna and I wanted to get everyone together to make sure we are all on the same page of what is going to be happening in the next week." He grabs her hand to hold before continuing on. "As you all know, Mason has left us. We will start the interviewing process this week for a new bodyguard and until we find one, Chase will be stepping in and accompanying Jenna and Avery wherever they go when I am not with them or if we are in a crowded setting." We all look over at Chase, who nods his head in agreement.

"We also have decided to start interviewing for a nanny, as well as house hunting since we seem to have outgrown this apartment." My shocked eyes find Jenna's and she mouths 'tomorrow', indicating she will fill me in with details then.

"I know everyone's schedules are busy, but Robert and Layla, I would really appreciate if you can help me with both the interviewing of a nanny and house hunting as I truly value your opinions," Jenna says, hope and excitement gleaming from her eyes.

"Since you're the one who determines my schedule, I feel I

have no choice in the matter," Robert responds with sarcasm and we all laugh at his joke.

"I will find the time for you," I confirm, as there is no way I am not helping my best friend out.

"Excellent, thank you!" Cal says with a smile. "We would also like both of you to accompany us to Vancouver when we tour Wilson Enterprises. We will make this trip both business and pleasure.

"Wait, why would we go and tour Chase's family business?" I ask Cal in confusion, not understanding what Chase's business has to do with us. I look between Cal and Chase, who seem to be having a silent battle of words brewing between them.

"I would have thought you would have told her considering the amount of time you two have been spending together these last couple of days," Cal says in a challenging voice while looking at Chase. I notice Chase lock his jaw, his hazel eyes narrowed in anger at Cal. *How does Cal know we have been spending time together,* I wonder. Cal raises his eyebrows at Chase, waiting for him to respond.

"What the hell is going on here?" I demand, queasiness starting to fill my stomach as thoughts of being used once again start to swirl within my head.

"Cal is interested in becoming an investor in my family's company." Chase confirms with no emotion in his voice.

Dread races through my veins and the sudden urge to run and get the hell away from Chase overtakes me. "Excuse me," I say as I throw down my napkin, push my chair back and storm out of the apartment. I ignore Chase calling after me until I reach the elevators and as I push the down button, he grabs my arm and whirls me around.

"Layla, wait! It isn't what you're thinking," he pleads as he grabs my arms and forces me to look at him.

"Really, Chase, because it's starting to feel like a sick sense of déjà vu all over again!" I huff, shaking off his arms with as much force as I can. He let's go of me and rakes a hand through his hair.

"Layla, I meant to tell you. It slipped my mind these last couple of days, as I was trying to make sure my full attention was solely focused on you."

"So, it slipped your mind when you were having a conference call with your brother the other night? Hard to imagine that the subject of Cal's visit wouldn't have been a topic of conversation," I say, my voice laced with angry sarcasm.

"Layla, Cal found out through a private investigator about my family's struggles. When I came to him last week with my two weeks' notice, HE made the offer to be an investor if I provided him with information on how I plan to re-build the company. I never sought Cal out about this, nor would I had ever in a million years considered him to be interested."

"Humor me for a second here. Was the plan to make me fall in love with you until Cal signed on the dotted line and then completely ignore and forget about me once you had his money back in Canada?" I ask in disgust, not believing he might be innocent in all of this.

"God damn it, Layla, what do I have to do to show you I am one hundred percent being honest with you? It never even entered my mind that you would react this way. I would have told you the minute after he offered it if I thought you would assume that I was using you to get to Cal!" He throws his hands up in the air in frustration, his eyes begging me to believe him. "When are you going to stop assuming the worse of me and start trusting me?"

"With your past track record, I don't know if I can ever trust you," I spit out the verbal dagger, hoping I hit my mark.

And with the hurt that immediately fills his eyes, it looks like I hit the bullseye.

We stare at each other in silence and when the bell of the

elevator's arrival sounds, he is the first one to break eye contact as he makes his way to the open doors.

"Well, I guess we have no foundation to build on. I apologize for wasting your, and my, time."

He walks into the elevator, pushes the ground floor button, and looks at me with icy coldness as the doors close.

22

LAYLA

My demons won out as soon as I left Jenna's apartment. I stopped at the liquor store before going home, bought a bottle of vodka and went back to my apartment to continue making bad decisions. I must have written Chase five different text messages, each one containing a different message. And I deleted each one before hitting the send button. I finally fell asleep after drinking half of the bottle straight, only to be woken up five hours later to throw up, my body revolting against the liquor.

And, here I continue to torture myself by meeting Jenna for a morning walk. She is going to want to talk about Chase, especially since I refused to do so when I came back into her apartment to retrieve my keys and she saw how upset I was. She begged me to spend the night and sleep on the couch, but I needed to get out of there to be alone. Maybe talking to Jenna about Chase will be therapeutic. Maybe she will affirm that I need to stay far away from him.

I see her waiting for me at our meeting place on the Lakefront Trail when I stop short to see that she is not alone this morning and that Chase is with her. They are not talking as he is standing a couple feet away from her, looking around, but the mere site of him raises my blood pressure in both a good and bad way.

"Fuck!" I yell out in frustration, not only from the hot coffee that just splashed all over my shirt and burned me, but also that I forgot he started his new job as temporary bodyguard for her. This means he will be with her every time I see her out. How am I supposed to talk about him when he is right there?

"Are you okay?" she asks running up to me, concern written all over her face.

"Yes, I just spilled coffee all over myself," I say, as I try to wipe the remaining wetness off me. He has followed Jenna, but turns his back on us once he sees that all is fine. Having him not ask me if I was okay stings and I was slightly disappointed that I didn't have any text messages from him apologizing again. With him ignoring us, I have a full view of his delicious backside incased in jogging pants, his muscles flexing underneath his white t-shirt. He's wearing sunglasses and his ear length hair is pulled into a high ponytail. He looks more like an incredibly hot personal trainer rather than the sexy bodyguard that he is temporarily portraying.

If he's going to ignore me, then I'm just going to ignore him as well!

"How are we going to talk about him if he's with us?" I whisper, while watching him to see if he heard me.

Jenna glances at him before giving me a bemused look. "I guess we aren't going to. Question, how do you plan on drinking hot coffee while we are speed walking?"

"Sorry, I just needed a pick me up this morning," I walk over to the trash can to throw my cup away.

"Yes, I can smell your hangover a mile away," she sarcastically replies as she pulls back from giving me a hug. I silently berate myself for not showering before I came here as it does not surprise me that she can smell the vodka sweating out of my pores.

"I had good reason to indulge last night," I respond in my

defense and notice Chase's back tense at this, indicating he is listening in on our conversation. Jenna watches him as well and then nods at me in acknowledgement.

"Chase, we will take the trail to Shedd Aquarium and then turn around to come back." Jenna instructs and he nods his head in agreement. We start to walk, Chase following us, positioned on Jenna's right side.

"Start spilling your guts about your trip," I demand, needing to be distracted from feeling Chase's eyes on me. "And don't tell me again how it was amazing, and the house Cal rented was gorgeous, blah, blah, blah. I want to know about what changed your mind about hiring a nanny and searching for a new house."

"Avery and I are gong back with him to Thailand. Cal and I both agree that we cannot be apart for more than a week. So, I will need a nanny who is also trained in homeschooling as Avery starts kindergarten in a couple of weeks."

"Avery is going to be homeschooled?" I ask in shock, not ever imaging that would be her life. Jenna and I always talked about how Avery would go to the same schools we did growing up.

"It's the only way," she sighs with resignation. "If we know our future schedules are keeping us here in Chicago for an entire school year, then she will go to private school. But since the unlikelihood of that is high, we will need a trained educator to help when we are on the road. It is easier if the nanny is also the homeschool teacher."

Everything that Jenna says makes sense, but I just nod my head in response, not trusting my voice as the thought of them not being in Chicago with me makes me want to cry. "And what about house hunting? What areas are you looking at? Winnetka?" Winnetka is one of the wealthiest suburbs in Chicago and would seem fitting for a person like Cal.

"I prefer to stay as close as I can get to the city, but yes, Winnetka, Oak Brook, Hinsdale, maybe Wilmette," She rattles off some other affluent suburbs. "I'm still not ruling out finding something else in the city either."

"What are you going to do with your apartment? Please don't tell me you are going to sell it." I beg, not bearing the thought of her giving up the precious gem that her grandmother left her. Jenna can be very sentimental, so the thought of her selling her apartment that has so many happy memories seems out of character of her.

"No, I'll never sell that place. We've decided to rent it out and even have our first tenant in mind."

"Really? Who?" I wonder, thinking that she is going to ask Robert in order to help him out financially.

"You," She says seriously and I stop in my tracks, my mouth hanging wide open in shock. "It's time, Layla. There's no reason for you to stay in your place with all those memories haunting you. You need a fresh start and since we've had so many good times in my place, I think it's the perfect place for you to start your new, healthier journey."

Tears cloud my vision and without being able to form any sentences at this moment, I fling myself on her and squeeze. I bury my face into her neck and cry out tears of gratitude as it feels like a huge weight has been lifted off my shoulders.

"I'm sorry!" I mumble as I pull out of our hug and wipe at my tears. I smile at her when I notice she's wiping her eyes as well. I look over at Chase to see he is standing farther back from us to try to give us some privacy.

"When will I move in?" The wheels start to turn in my brain, needing facts in order to start packing and to take time off of work.

"We are going to start packing up now and move all of our stuff into storage the day before we leave for Thailand," she confirms as we start walking again.

"Wait, that's in less than two weeks! You won't be able to find and move into a new house by then!"

"We can rent a place or live in a hotel until we find the perfect house," she shrugs her shoulders nonchalantly, as if none of this is a big deal.

"Wow, I truly can't believe this," I say in awe and feel the need to pinch myself to make sure I am not dreaming. "Now if I can only get a new job, things really will be on a better path for me."

"Yeah, Robert told me all about Torrin Richards and the House of Royalty. Both he and the club have a notorious reputation. Robert also indulged me on the story of how you and Mr. Richards originally met." She looks at me with a smirk that causes me to laugh.

"You always tell me not to judge a book by its cover, Jenna. Maybe all those rumors you hear are from jealous people." I chide, giving her a dose of her own medicine.

"Maybe so, but with Robert calling him a dangerously sexy, large dose of cocaine that you want to sexually shoot up, I would say the cover might be judged accurately."

I shake my head at Robert's gossiping. "It's only a job interview. We'll see if I get asked for a second one. Now..." I decide it is time to change subjects and get to an important task on hand that she hasn't mentioned yet. "Why are you not wearing the gorgeous engagement ring Cal made for you?"

She starts to laugh and doesn't seem surprised that I know. "I was wondering when you were going to ask me about it."

"How did you know I knew?" Surprise laces my voice, as I didn't think Cal was going to tell her he asked for my permission.

"Because when I said no, Cal grumbled 'Bloody hell, she was right' and it made me put two and two together." I laugh at this as I can picture Cal saying those exact words.

"What did you tell him your reasoning for saying no was?" I ask, curiosity getting the best of me.

"I told him I needed to see how we're going to handle the next month on location with him. He told me he didn't understand why that had to change the dynamic of our relationship."

"What did you say to that?" I ask, as I completely agree with Cal.

"I said that if I can't handle being on location with him, then we might not be able to stay together."

"And what did he say to that?" I probe, needing her to tell me everything that transpired during their conversation.

"He told me that he would give up acting if I was unhappy because he refuses to have a life without me and Avery." She gives me a shy smile, but the happiness of it all is radiating from her eyes.

"So, what did you say?" I softly ask, enjoying seeing my best friend so very happy.

"I told him to ask me again once he is done shooting the movie." She gives me a sly smile with a wink.

"EEK!" I screech in excitement as we grab each other's hands and start bouncing up and down in a circle like two little kids. Once we stop circling, I turn to Chase to see if he heard the good news but stop myself as I see his stoic face turn to ignore us once I look in his direction.

You miss him, the angel on my left shoulder says.

I smile at the mental image of punching the angel in the face.

23

CHASE

I thought being Jenna's bodyguard was going to be easy compared to being a paparazzi. I was dead wrong - it is so much more mentally and physically exhausting. I accompany Jenna everywhere she goes, starting at seven in the morning, until at least six in the evening. My day doesn't stop once I get her home safely as Cal then wants to meet with me to discuss the events of the day and then switches gears to discuss every single financial aspect of the winery. He doesn't want to be in Vancouver for very long - just a couple of days - so he is demanding to view the hard numbers now and all visual presentations and tours can happen in Vancouver. By the time I get home, my body falls into bed from exhaustion.

But, my mind keeps me up with thoughts on Layla.

It has been three long, agonizing days since our fight and I don't know how to handle it. Her telling me she still doesn't trust me was a knife to my heart and I don't know how to show her my sincerity. Part of me wants to shake some sense into her, but the other part says she needs more time. I see her almost every single day and it physically hurts to not kiss or hold her. Yesterday, I had to sit at the bar while her and Jenna met for lunch to celebrate her getting the new job at the House of Royalty. It took every ounce of will power not to smash my glass of water at the thought of that scumbag being her new boss.

"She's not ready yet, Chase."

Jenna's voice retrieves me out of the trance that thoughts of Layla always put me in. We are in her office, interviewing nanny candidates. Robert and Layla are helping, but stepped out to pick up food for lunch. I look down at our schedule of interviews and then back at the time, noting we still have hour to kill. "Of course the next candidate isn't ready yet. You were quick to cut the last interview short, clearly being obvious that you had no further desire to continue on with your questioning." Jenna has a list of required questions we ask the candidates. The last candidate was a rock star on paper, but not very impressive in person. I was happy Jenna didn't waste our time by continuing on with them.

"I'm not talking about the next candidate. I'm talking about Layla." Jenna looks me straight in the eye, knowing she has piqued my interest with this topic of conversation.

"What makes you think she's not ready? What if she is, but she's just scared?" I challenge as it is easy to hide behind excuses when you are scared.

"Of course, she's scared. She's scared because you've stirred feelings up inside of her. I see the change in her. She hasn't responded to anyone like the way she's responded to you. But for some reason, she wants to bury her newfound feelings instead of embracing them." She sighs and shakes her head. "I'm afraid if you keep pushing her, it will be in the wrong direction."

"Why are you helping me with Layla?" I look at her with suspicion since she's Layla's best friend and would only want the best for her.

"Because I like you, Chase. I think you would be very good for her."

"So what do you suggest, Jenna? I can't fight for someone who refuses to trust me. We will just keep going around in circles."

She gets out of her chair to look at the view out of her window. She contemplates her answer before turning around to answer me. "I think you need to temporarily let her go," she says so softly that at first I don't think I hear her correctly.

"What? How in the hell would that help me gain her trust?" I stare at her, thinking her exhaustion is setting in as this sounds like the craziest idea ever.

"You're going to be her friend - NO texting every morning, NO kissing, NO dates. You will apologize to her one more time and stop ignoring her, but also don't be in her business. And you will especially stop following her."

I sit back, cross my arms over my chest and scowl at her, not liking any of these suggestions. I am a grown, fucking man and know how to woo over a woman. It's just taking me longer with one as complicated as Layla.

"As of right now, she's refusing to go to Vancouver. I'll convince her otherwise as will you. You will ask her to come as a FRIEND! And when we leave, you'll let her go without a shred of guilt or a promise of keeping in touch."

"Hell no, Jenna! I don't know how long it's going to take to get my business up and running comfortably again. It could take a year! I'm not going to go that long without talking to her." I slam my hand against the table in anger, causing one of Jenna's new assistants to jump in her seat and look back at me.

"She needs to live this new life she's finally having the courage to start! She needs to be distraction-free in order to see your value and that you are not trying to use her. She needs to date other people to see what she's missing out on by not having you."

The thought of another man's hands on Layla makes my blood boil and I ball my hands into fists. "No, Jenna. Absolutely not!" I growl, refusing to acknowledge her words.

She looks up at the door to see the lock being twisted, indicating that they have arrived back. She leans over the table and gets close to my face, making sure she holds eye contact with me.

"You need to go back to Canada and work your ass off. Concentrate only on YOU, Chase. Heal yourself, heal your family and get your business running. Once that is done, you then come here to win her heart. Think about it because your way isn't working; she is NOT ready!"

We stare at each other in a silent challenge before she breaks eye contact and goes back to sit down in her seat.

"Everything okay in here? The air seems to be filled with lots of tension," Robert asks as he unloads the bag of Chinese food. Layla helps him, refusing to make eye contact with me as she hands me my food.

"Everything is great!" Jenna says a little too enthusiastically, a clear indicator that she is lying.

"Hmm…I don't really believe you, but whatever," Robert says in his know-it-all voice. "The next candidate is sitting in the hallway. She says her flight arrived early, so she decided to come straight here."

"This is the one that flew in from France and is a family friend of Sean and his family," Jenna says, referring to Cal's best friend and famous actor, Sean Lindsey. Jenna picks up her resume from her pile of candidates to review. "Isla Jones. She speaks four languages and has spent the last three years with the family of a British diplomat in Paris. She received her education in child development and is certified to homeschool. She also plays the piano." She looks up with an impressed expression on her face. "She almost sounds too good to be true."

"I wonder why she's not with the British diplomat anymore," I ask out loud and all three of them look at me in agreement.

"Well, we can't hire her despite how good she sounds," Robert says and we all look at him in questioning. "She is hot. Like hot for teacher hot. You don't hire hot nannies."

Jenna rolls her eyes while Layla can't keep back her giggle. The sound makes my dick stand to attention and I immediately grind my teeth in annoyance.

"You know, now that I think about it, she does kind of resemble Cora, but a much nerdier Cora," Layla says, as she taps her finger against her lips in thought. I stare at those lips a little too long, not caring that she just caught me looking at her. Cora Gregory is a Hollywood actress who went to the same boarding school as Cal and Sean. She is gorgeous with long dark hair and cat like green eyes. She is one of Hollywood's most beautiful leading ladies, but tends to only get parts due to her physical appearance and not her acting abilities.

"Hopefully she doesn't have the same temperament as Cora," Jenna says. I distinctly remember hearing the story that Cora is in love with Cal, despite his devotion to Jenna and Jenna is now her number one enemy. "We can reheat our food after the interview. Robert, please welcome her in."

"But I'm hungry!" Robert whines while stomping his foot like a child.

"It is rude and unprofessional to leave her out there while we eat. You can eat while we interview her if you really want," Jenna looks at him with a raised eyebrow, daring him to do it.

"Of course, you would want me to look like the asshole," he grumbles as he heads to the door to bring Isla in for the interview.

After dropping Jenna off at her apartment for the evening, I decided to take the long way home and walk to clear my mind and think about Jenna's advice on Layla. Fortunately Cal was still interviewing potential new bodyguards so I was able to slip out before he had the chance to keep me there for another three hours of talking. I don't like Jenna's advice, but the more I contemplate it, the more I see she has a point. I decide a truce is in order and go straight to the flower shop to buy some flowers for Layla and wait for her outside her apartment building, hoping that will force her to see me.

One hour later, I see her heading toward me. She hasn't noticed me yet as her head is down looking at the sidewalk while walking. She looks exhausted and I wonder if I'm the cause of it. I decide to stand a few feet in front of the glass doors in order for her to notice me. She glances up and then does a double take, her eyes widening in shock at the sight of me.

"Hello Ang…I mean, Layla," I smile at her, mentally telling myself I need to refrain from calling her 'angel' if I'm only going to be her friend. "I have come to beg for forgiveness and ask that you reconsider my friendship." I hand her the first bouquet of flowers to take. "These are for you as a peace offering. I'm so very sorry you felt the way you did by my omission of Cal's interest in my winery. I told you before that I would never betray you and I meant that. Whether you want to believe me or not is your choice."

"The next bouquet are congratulatory flowers on your new job. I wish you nothing but success in your new endeavor." I lie threw my teeth as I hand her the second bouquet because I would like nothing more than the House of Royalty nightclub to go under in order for Layla to not be working with Torrin Richards.

A gorgeous hue of pink tints her cheeks as she blushes. "Thank you, Chase. The flowers are beautiful and I really do appreciate the apology." She gives me a sad smile and struggles with what she wants to say next. I hold up my hand as she starts to talk again, not wanting her to say something that contradicts what she feels due to her being scared. I know I cloud her judgment just as much as she clouds mine. I still feel the electric spark between us and hope comes back alive for me knowing she still feels it too.

"You don't need to say anything to me, Layla. Just know that I'm trying to be a friend. I look forward to seeing you soon." Despite my better judgment, I give her a swift kiss on the cheek and force myself to walk away without turning back.

24

LAYLA

One Week Later

The view of the Pacific Northwest from thirty-thousand feet is breathtaking with clear blue skies and what seems to be an endless range of mountain tops. Chicago is so flat compared to this part of the country that I'm mesmerized by the sights. The peacefulness of the view and the soothing noise of the jet engines help calm my nerves.

As I sit here on this private, luxury jet that Cal has chartered, I do wonder *what in the hell am I doing here*? I have no business being here, but when Jenna told me that they were accompanying Cal back to Thailand straight from Vancouver, I panicked at the thought of not having time with her before she left. Since I gave my two weeks' notice at work already, I used up my remaining vacation time to spend this last week packing up my apartment, selling my furniture and then helping Jenna pack up their personal belongings in order to be officially moved in when I return from Vancouver. Packing up my apartment was cathartic. I purged everything and the only items that I have of Charlie are photographs and memories. I didn't cry when I looked around the empty apartment for the last time. Instead, I smiled and held my head high as I locked the door and gave the key back to the landlord. The decision to finally leave felt right.

Fortunately, Jenna is not a hoarder and already had a lot of her non-every day items in storage. With the help of professional packers, the rest of their personal items were officially moved into storage yesterday. Before we left this morning, I moved in my clothes and the small amount of decor items I kept, which wasn't much as I plan on starting fresh and buying whatever items I need that Jenna is not supplying me. She is letting me use all of her furniture since Cal promised she can decorate the new house whatever way she wanted.

I look over at her sitting next to Robert and start to get a little teary eyed at the thought of not seeing her for a month. As if she can sense I'm watching her, she looks up, smiles and winks at me. She and Robert have been strategizing on what she is going to work on while being overseas. I don't see this being a huge change for her, as her work load of being more involved with clients started to lighten as soon as Avery was born. Robert has become more of the face of the company, with Jenna concentrating on running it behind the scenes.

While she and Robert work, Avery and her new nanny, Isla, play a board game. Avery liked Isla within a minute after meeting her and so far, it seems to be a perfect match. I still get a weird vibe at how dismissive Isla was during her interview regarding the last couple she worked for, but obviously Jenna didn't have an issue with it and hired her after her background check cleared.

My gaze wonders over to where Cal and Chase are sitting. They are discussing the itinerary for Vancouver with James, Jenna's new bodyguard. James has more experience with being a celebrity bodyguard than Mason did and while he is not as good looking as Mason, he has interacted more with all of us in one week than Mason did in almost one year.

I close my eyes as I listen to Chase describe to James the

venues that we will be visiting. I inhale a deep breath and recall vividly my latest dreams of him, which causes me to cross my legs as heat pools in between them. He has stayed true to his word about only trying to be my friend, but one that doesn't call or text you. I catch him staring at me sometimes, his eyes so heated with the same desire that I've been craving from him, but he has not acted on his desire and has stayed away from me. His actions have left me disappointed. I open up my eyes and stare at him, realization hitting me smack in the face.

I want the old Chase back.

I don't want to just be Chase's friend.

I want those morning text messages.

I want to hear him call me Angel.

I want those damn kisses that are molten lava to my core.

But news of him staying behind in Vancouver once Cal and Jenna depart has left me feeling unsettled. How can I feel this way for someone who will no longer be in the same city as me? We both have the means to try to make long distance work, but do I want to even try? Would he still even want to try?

The captain's voice breaks into my thoughts as he announces we will be landing in Vancouver shortly. Cal, Chase and James continue on with their conversation while Jenna and Robert pack up their laptops and stop working. They join Avery, Isla and I near the window to look at the beautiful city of Vancouver surrounded by mountains and water. Twenty minutes later, the plane wheels smoothly touch down and we have officially landed at Vancouver International Airport. Because we are on a private chartered plane, we stop near a private hanger where a large black Mercedes passenger van awaits for us to disembark from the plane.

"Everyone, I want to welcome you to Vancouver! Our transportation is here to take us to the house you will be staying at for the next couple of days. We will settle in and relax for a couple of hours before having dinner," Chase instructs as we unbuckle our seat belts and head towards the stairway to get off the plane. The air is filled with excitement as most of us have never been to Vancouver before and are looking forward to the adventure that awaits us.

Chase plays tour guide for us during our forty-five minute car ride, pointing out some famous sites of downtown Vancouver. Our route then leads us into Stanley Park and over the gorgeous Lions Gate Bridge as we head into West Vancouver. As if I wasn't already in awe over how magnificent the city was, I wasn't prepared for the beauty of the French Chateau that is going to be our home away from home for the next four days.

"Pinch me...pinch me so fucking hard because I think I am dreaming," Robert says, as we step through the doors of the mansion to see it is on the waterfront. Chase introduces us to Deborah, a kind looking, older woman who is the executive assistant at Wilson Enterprises. She secured the house for us and gives a tour, showing us the bedrooms, gym, movie room, and kitchen. She leads us back outside to the pool, where there is a large table with chairs and umbrella decked out with food and beverages for us to consume while we enjoy the waterfront view. We all sit down, completely famished from the plane ride, and start to eat.

"Deborah has made itineraries for everyone during your time here. While Cal and I tour the vineyard tomorrow, the rest of you will go sightseeing. Deborah has listed some of the top destinations to see in Vancouver. Just let Deborah know what time you will want to start tomorrow and the van will be here for you." Chase hands Jenna and Robert her card for them to call. I stare dumbfounded at this new Chase I don't recognize. I don't know why I didn't notice his attire on the plane, but he is wearing a beautifully tailored suit with no tie, his hair worn down and styled. As much as I love seeing him in casual clothes, there is something dangerously sexy about a man in a suit. Since we are on his turf, he oozes an air of control, combined with power, but not in a conceited way. I blink a couple of times, never dreaming about seeing him in this light and I am beyond turned on.

"Now, if you will excuse me everyone, Deborah and I will leave for you to settle in. We will be back tonight for dinner with more of the staff that we would like for you to meet. Enjoy the rest of your day and we will see you later." He nods at Deborah, who gets up to leave with him. I hesitate on whether or not to go after him, but with the reminder that my time with him is limited, I decide to go after him.

"Chase!" I yell, running after him and Deborah. He turns around at the sound of my voice, surprise registering on his face at my wanting his attention.

"Hi…um, your city is beautiful," I stammer, not knowing how to start off this conversation with him and feeling like a bumbling idiot.

"Thank you." He smiles and looks back at Deborah. "Deborah, I'll meet you in the car." She nods her head and turns to leave. "Is there something you need, Layla?" Chase asks, concern on his face.

"Are you staying here with us?" I swallow, not understanding why I am being so shy all of a sudden as I have always been the dominate personality when it came to men.

"No, I'm staying at my condo." He gives me a questioning look as to why I wanted to know.

"Oh, okay. Well, if there's some time tonight after dinner…I… um, would like to talk with you privately." *What in the hell is wrong with you, Layla? Be confident!*

"Sure we can. Are you okay, Angel?" He asks as he studies my flushed cheeks.

"Yes!" I say enthusiastically at hearing him use my nickname again. "Yes, I'm great!"

"Okay, good." He takes my hand and squeezes it. "I'll see you later then." And he departs without looking back.

Later that evening, Chase returned with his brother, Rhys, and some important key players of Wilson Enterprises. We all sit outside for dinner, where a chef and a staff of six serves us a five course meal. Dinner consisted mostly of casual talk, with Chase doing most of the talking to try to ease the two sides of his world together. Rhys quietly observed everyone from afar, his face showing no emotions as he assessed each one of us when we played an ice breaker game that their Director of Marketing suggest we play in order to get to know one another better. Four hours later, dinner was starting to wind down. Jenna and Cal excused themselves and said good night to everyone in order to put Avery to bed, who fell asleep in Jenna's lap. Rhys and the rest of the Wilson Enterprises staff said their goodbyes and left. Robert persuaded Isla and James to go play a round of pool with him, sensing that I needed time alone with Chase. As soon as everyone was out of ear shot, I got up and sat closer to him.

"Thank you so much for a beautiful evening. Did you orchestrate all of this for us?"

He shrugs his shoulders, as if none of this is a big deal. "I just had a vision of what I wanted and Deborah made it happen. You are going to have an amazing time tomorrow with what she has planned."

"Chase…"I start, needing to rip the band aid off and tell him what I am feeling. "I want to see your world. I want to see your offices, see your home, meet your friends. I really want to understand you better while we are here in your world."

He closes his eyes, his expression pained as he tries to find his next words. "Layla, I can't keep letting you in only, to have you push me out every time I make a mistake." He bites his lip and I sense that he is nervous for revealing that to me.

Revealing that I'm the one who actually has the power to hurt him as much as he has the power to hurt me.

I take both of his hands, settle them onto my lap and squeeze them in reassurance. "I want to try, Chase. I know you're a good man and I trust you don't want to hurt me. I don't want to hurt you either. So, if you aren't interested in me anymore, I completely understand." I look down at our hands as he maneuvers them so that he is the one now gripping mine instead of me gripping his.

"I will forever be interested in you, Layla," he growls and the intensity of his voice causes me to look up at him. In one swift motion, he swoops his head down and sears me with his lips. I wrap my arms around his neck and throw myself into his lap, needing to feel him against me. His tongue demands entrance into my mouth and I am more than happy to oblige. I moan out loud from his delicious taste, my hands holding his head to mine so I can deepen the kiss as our tongues thrust into each other. His hand moves to my breast and starts to slowly caress my nipple through the fabric of my dress. So lost am I in him, his touch, his noises - that I don't feel the vibration of his phone. When he pulls his mouth away from mine, I whimper at the loss, my head screaming to distract him away from his phone. I start nipping at his neck, leaving a trail of scorching kisses with my tongue back to his mouth. He pulls his phone out of his pocket just as I feel those lips back on mine and for a brief moment, my brain screams victory. It's only when he doesn't kiss me back with his normal enthusiastic passion that I realize the moment is gone and fizzled as he is distracted by whatever he is reading on his phone.

He presses his forehead against mine while trying to regain his composure. Disappointment runs through my veins and cools my blood that his kisses had lit on fire. My breathing slows down as I wait for him to speak.

"Angel, I'm sorry, but I need to go," he sighs out his own disappointment and leans back so he can look me in the eyes. "I wish I didn't, but my brother needs me to head back to the office."

"Now? But it's almost eleven o'clock at night," I ask incredulously, not believing that he is going to work now.

"I know, but he wants to go over the itinerary for tomorrow and this is the only time to do it. I'm sorry. Tomorrow is going to be a long day for everyone. Promise me you will have dinner with me? Alone?" His eyes plead with me to understand, the emotion unnecessary as I'm ecstatic that he still wants me.

"Absolutely." I nod and give him a soft kiss on the lips. I get off of him and smooth out my dress that is now wrinkled from his roaming hands.

"Walk me to my car?" He doesn't give me a chance to answer as he gets up, takes my hand and heads toward the house. He kisses me two more times before he leaves, one of those times coming dangerously close to us having sex on the hood of his car. I watch him drive away, leaving me breathless with hopes for tomorrow.

25

CHASE

My heart is hammering in my chest from the adrenaline that is buzzing through my body as I watch Cal sign on the dotted line; his letter of intent to become our first investor and celebrity endorser in the history of Wilson Enterprises. We had transportation pick up Cal and his agent separately this morning, in order to meet us at a hanger for the chartered helicopters we rented to take us to the vineyard. The forty-five minute helicopter ride east provided gorgeous views of the mountains that cascade through British Columbia and Washington State. Once we landed, we spent all day touring the vineyard with the Chief of Staff, who meticulously explained each and every detail that goes into the making of our most famous commodity - our ice wine. After meetings and lunch filled with samplings of our wines, we took the helicopters back to Vancouver to have more meetings at headquarters. Cal was gracious and shook every single employee's hand, signed autographs and took photos with them before we were able to isolate him in more meetings, that included marketing and advertising plans for him, and repeating the content of the contract we had previously sent to his lawyers and accountants for approval a couple of days ago. Once adjustments on numbers of profit revenue sharing were corrected, it only took Cal and his agent to have a ten minute private discussion before announcing his verbal agreement to our terms. We went over the updated itinerary for the next couple of days as we will now do a press conference at the vineyard and have a private party in downtown Vancouver, inviting the most influential people in British Columbia and the people who are on the list as other potential investors that Rhys and I have on our wishlist.

We walk Cal and his agent back to the awaiting transportation and watch in silence as they leave our offices. Once their cars are out of sight, Rhys and I turn to look at each other and I stare at him in amazement as genuine excitement is radiating from his eyes.

"I can't believe that just happened. We did it - we fucking did it!" He shouts and before I can answer, he is hugging me tightly. I wrap my arms around him in return, savoring this moment with him as brotherly moments like this are few and far between. "I feel like I just scored five goals," he laughs as we break apart and walk back to our offices.

"Enjoy this feeling, baby brother. All your hard work in saving our family's business is going to pay off," I reassure him, wanting him to feel as proud of himself as I am of him.

"No, Chase. You sealed this deal. We might have physically arranged everything, but it was your vision, your knowledge of the vineyard, your confidence and savvy business skills of putting the deal together. We could never have pulled this off without you." His acknowledgement of my hard work means the world to me as I busted my ass on this deal and to see it come to fruition sparked that passion that I once had for Wilson Enterprises. I've missed this place. I've missed the employees. I feel valued and respected here - two emotions that you will never find in the paparazzi business. This is where I belong and with the outcome of today, I know I am needed in order to bring success back to the family business.

I belong here and the feeling calms any anxiety I had of returning home.

Where does that leave Layla?

Shit I forgot about dinner with Layla!

So caught up in the emotions of the day, that I lost track of time. When I look at my watch for the time, I am shocked to see it is past eight p.m. I excuse myself from my brother and race back to my office to find three missed text messages within the last four hours from her:

Layla: Are we still on for dinner tonight? If so, what are the plans?

Layla: Hope you are okay since I haven't heard from you.

Layla: Couldn't wait anymore for dinner. Enjoy your evening.

I quickly rattle off a text to her, asking her to pick up when I call in five seconds as I know she won't if she is mad at me. I hit send, count to five very slowly and call her.

"Angel, I am so sorry," I say as soon as she answers. "With Cal agreeing to the contract tonight, we had to quickly call all the vendors we had on hold to give them the green light for the events we are going to have during the next two days announcing our partnership with him."

"So, you are still at the office?" She questions, her voice sounding less angry from when she previously barked 'hello' at me.

"Yes, Angel. I'm still here. We have some more work to go over before I can leave. I didn't realize I left my cell phone in my office until I saw the time and how late it was. If I send a car for you, would you come to my condo tonight when I am done?" I plead in a husky voice, my need to see her overtaking my thoughts.

"I'm already snuggled up with Avery, watching a movie."

Disappointment laces through me, but it is my fault for not getting in touch with her sooner.

"I understand. No excuses tomorrow, I promise. Tell me about your day," I ask, not ready to hang up yet as I am curious about her thoughts on Vancouver.

"It was a wonderful day. I think we hit up every major tourist attraction in Vancouver. Avery loved the aquarium. I can't get over how beautiful it is here," she marvels and I love hearing her appreciation for the city I call home.

"Do you think you could ever see yourself here?" The need to know if she would ever be willing to move here for me is overwhelming.

"Never say never, Chase. Leaving Chicago always seemed like an inconceivable idea to me. But, now I can see that it isn't anymore." I smile at her answer, those words exactly what I needed to hear. "Tell me how your day was? When Cal returned, he told us all about your beautiful vineyard and seemed excited about the partnership."

"Today was long and tiring, but absolutely amazing. The team has worked so hard to show Cal what an elite partnership it would be and it looks like their hard work has paid off. I am so proud of my brother and everyone who has worked such late hours."

"I can hear it in your voice how elated and proud you are. But Chase, you were part of this too. Be proud of yourself!" She encourages and I shake my head in wonder at her support, despite me standing her up tonight.

"Thank you, Angel. I am proud of myself. I felt alive today and it made me realize how I've missed being part of the business. Seeing all of our loyal employees who I have worked side by side with for a long time. It felt really good to be back. I honestly didn't think once about my father," I admit to her and to myself for the first time since being back home.

"I am genuinely happy for you, Chase. Have you seen your mother yet?" She asks tentatively.

"No, not yet. Tomorrow will be the first time as she will be at the press conference. You will get to meet her too."

"It's okay if I don't," she says quickly, which causes me to laugh.

"You are important to me, Angel, so therefore, you will meet her," I confirm, making sure she isn't caught by surprise when I make the introductions.

"Hmmm," she says in a sleepy mumble and I realize it's late for her with the two hour time change.

"Go to sleep, Angel. I will see you in your dreams." We say good night and I continue to work. I don't want anything to stand in my way of having alone time with her tomorrow night.

26

LAYLA

The day starts out early as we all have to wake up around seven in the morning to get ready for today's press conference. I choose my attire wisely as I want to look professional, yet chic since I am here to support Cal and Jenna, but I also want to make sure I look good for meeting Chase's mother. We were told to bring numerous outfits for multiple events and even though I overpacked, I still feel unprepared. With help from Robert, I decide to wear emerald satin green tuxedo style pants, a warm black turtle neck sweater and a stylish black trench coat since it is chilly here. Black suede wedges round out my look to be comfortable to walk around in. I finish my hair and make up and join everyone in the kitchen to grab breakfast before going to the vineyard.

Once breakfast is completed, we climb into the van and are driven back to the private jet terminal at Vancouver International Airport. A chartered plane is waiting for our arrival, with Chase, his brother and a group of people all outside waiting to greet us. I take a deep breath and look outside my window to see Cal shaking hands with everyone and introducing Jenna and Avery to them. Chase and Rhys are standing next to a stunning older woman who Rhys favors, but I can tell Chase inherited her cheekbones. Lara Wilson is the epitome of sophistication and I suddenly feel inadequate to meet her.

"Layla, are you okay?" Robert turns back to look at me before exiting the van, noticing my pale complexion.

"Yes, just tired," I respond, not wanting Robert to know how nervous I am to meet Chase's mother. Despite Chase and I not officially being a couple, her opinion of me really does matter. I stand up and smooth out my already wrinkled pants. I take one more look out of the window and notice a tall, beautiful red head standing next to Chase's mom. As Chase introduces Cal and Jenna to his mother, this woman watches him with a certain type of pride that only someone who is close would show publicly.

"Robert, do you know who that red-headed woman is?" Robert did all the research on the people he would be meeting, so I am curious if he knows who she is.

"You mean the enchanting goddess standing next to Lara Wilson? That is Ellory Davis, daughter to Roger Davis, one of the richest families in Canada. Apparently Chase's father and Roger were close, even trying to arrange a marriage between Chase and Ellory when they dated in college."

I fall back into my seat in shock, not prepared by the news that I am meeting one of Chase's former girlfriends.

"Why are you looking like that? She is not a threat - they aren't together anymore. You really need to start stalking people that come into your life, Layla." He chides and I nod my head in agreement.

"So everyone tells me," I sarcastically respond and take another look at Ellory. "She is beautiful," I murmur, deep in my thoughts of wondering why Chase is still not with her.

"And so are you. Suck it up, buttercup! Get your ass out of that seat and let's go be the ballers that we are!" Robert heads out of the van and leaves me alone with my thoughts.

Why hasn't Chase mentioned her?

What does it matter that he didn't?

Does he still have feelings for her?

"There you are," Chase says as he gets into the van, looking for me. I flash him a smile, not wanting him to sense that anything is wrong. He looks divine in another dark colored suit with a white button down dress shirt underneath his blazer. His hair is styled again and the air permeates with his delicious Armani cologne. "Ready to meet everyone?" I nod my head and reach for the hand he has offered me. He pulls me into a hug, sending shivers up my spine as he nuzzles my neck.

"Damn, you smell good, Angel." He traces light kisses against my neck, up along my check and finally plants his lips on mine softly. I give him a quick kiss back and pull away, not wanting to be seen by anyone from the outside.

"You look amazing." His gaze slowly travels up and down my body with heated appreciation. Suddenly, the van has turned into a sauna, making me want to rip off all my clothes - and his as well. "C'mon, I want to introduce you to everyone."

He grabs my hand and leads the way off the van. I try to remove my hand from his, but he holds tightly as he walks straight to introduce me to his mother…and Ellory.

"Mother, this is Layla Sands, Jenna's best friend. Layla, this is my mother, Lara." Chase introduces us, his smile beaming on his face. He must have had a long talk with her because unconditional love is shining from her eyes as she gazes at her son.

"It is so nice to meet you, Mrs. Wilson." I extend my hand out, but she surprises me by grabbing me into a hug and kissing me on both sides of my cheeks.

"Chase has been raving about you, Layla, so the pleasure is all mine. He told us you were beautiful, but his words do not do you justice." Her words render me speechless as I was not prepared for such kindness. My cheeks feel like they are on fire from my bashfulness at her compliments and all I can muster out is a thank you back to her.

"Hi Layla, I am Ellory. It is so wonderful to finally meet you. Chase told me so much about you!" Ellory says with an overabundance of enthusiasm. *But Chase has said nothing about you, Ellory,* my mind screams as she squeezes my hand in a firm handshake. "We must find some time to talk and get to know one another. I would love to get some advice on your favorite places to go in Chicago as I'm hoping for a visit sometime soon."

"Sure, I would love that," I respond, adding another note to my mental checklist to research both Chase AND Ellory.

"Excuse me for interrupting, but I need to say hello to my little minx." A rich, masculine accented voice speaks behind me. I turn around to see who they are talking about, only to be surprised to find myself embraced in a strong hug from the devilishly handsome, Sean Lindsey.

"Sean! What are you doing here?" I laugh as I hug him back, missing his sexy Irish self. Sean is Cal's best friend and I met him in Las Vegas when I went to visit Jenna the same time she met Cal. I tried my hardest to seduce Sean, but he never took me up on my offer and now we have more like a brother/sister relationship.

"I came out to support Cal and to see if this venture is worth my money as well." I am about to respond to him when I feel myself hauled up next to Chase's hard body as he puts his arm possessively around my waist, making sure his territory is marked. He holds out his free hand for Sean to shake.

"Hi, I'm Chase Wilson." Chase's usual warm voice is ice cold as he sizes Sean up.

Sean does the same, a cruel smile appearing on his lips. "I know exactly who you are as I clearly remember you being a low-life paparazzi." Sean takes Chase's hand and leans in close to his ear. "Hurt my girl and I will ruin you," Sean says, in a low menacing tone before giving Chase a cold smile, dropping his hand and walking away.

Embarrassment creeps up along my cheeks and I look around to see who else had witnessed that exchange. The only person I see watching us is Isla, who has a surprising glint in her eyes as she watches Sean introduce himself to the Wilson Enterprises' staff. My intuition is telling me there is more to the story of them just being family friends.

"Chase, we need to get going," Rhys says, as he starts to usher everyone to board the plane. Chase drops his arm from around my waist and turns to me.

"My brother is going to need me to conduct business the rest of the day, but as soon as this press conference is over, you're mine," he growls, pecks me on the cheek and walks over to his mother to escort her on the plane.

I cover the area of my cheek where he had just kissed with my hand and look around for witnesses. Of course, the only people watching me like a hawk are Jenna and Robert, both of them staring at me with shit eating grins on their faces. I shake my head and laugh as I know they're going to interrogate me as soon as we have alone time.

Our day at the vineyard started out with a private tour, lunch at the restaurant on the property, and then ending with the press conference. Cal, Chase and Rhys talked about their partnership, answered questions for forty-five minutes, and then obliged all photography requests. By the time we were done, the early evening sky was speckled with gorgeous hues of purple, pink and blue as the sun was ready to set. The plane ride back to Vancouver was filled with excitement over the success of the press conference and anticipation for the gala the following evening. I start to panic a little at the thought of not having anything formal to wear, but Jenna reassures me that Cal has flown in his stylist and make up artist to take care of us.

As the plane gets closer to the city, trepidation starts to lace through my veins at the idea of being alone with Chase. Seeing him in his element confirms that he belongs here with his family. He needs to work on getting the business back to where it was and improving his relationship with both his mother and brother. Yesterday my thoughts were veering toward giving us a chance, but today is a different story.

Today I realize that I need to let him go.

Just like he needs to let me go.

I don't know if this will be temporary and will turn into something permanent, but we both have work to do on ourselves that needs to take priority over everything else. Chase may think he is ready to dive right into a relationship, but I see the importance of saving his business and family. I don't think he realizes that it is not something that is fixed over night. It takes time, focus and hard work. Now that my head is clearer, with my focus on learning how to respect and love myself again, I need to concentrate on my future, regardless of whether or not he is in it.

I watch him a couple of rows away from me, going over last minute details of tomorrow's party. He is commanding everyone's attention with his firm, confident voice, dictating his expectations to them. They nod and listen, glancing at him with respect. This is what he was meant to do. It is where he belongs.

But for the next forty-eight hours, I want him to be mine.

I want to forget about our limited time with each other.

I want to forget about our painful pasts.

I want to forget about how we originally started off.

I want to be lost…lost in him.

His handsome face is listening intently to one of his employees when his beautiful eyes unexpectedly meet mine. I stare at him in raw hunger, trying to communicate to him how much I want him. Understanding dawns on him as his face softens, eyes widen and his soft lips part as a tiny whisper of a breath escapes him. I am rewarded with the most tantalizing of smiles as the heat in his gaze promises me that he plans on fulfilling all of my desires tonight.

When the captain announces that we will be landing shortly, I tell Robert and Jenna my plans to leave with Chase since he wants to give me a tour of downtown, which considering he lives in downtown Vancouver, is not necessarily a lie. Jenna gives me a smirk, clearly not believing me, while Robert decides to be his usual sarcastic self. "I bet it is a private tour of *his* downtown," he snickers at his joke while I roll my eyes at him despite his accuracy that I one hundred percent without a doubt plan on touring Chase's 'downtown' area.

I can tell Chase has told his brother that he will not be returning back to the office because as Chase whispers his plans into his ear, Rhys' cold gaze lands on me disapprovingly. Harsh words are hushed out to one another and Rhys drops the matter, since Chase is not going to give in. I refuse to feel guilty about taking Chase away from work as I only have limited hours with him, whereas Rhys will have him forever.

The plane makes a smooth landing and comes to a stop when we reach the private charter hanger. I walk off with everyone, quickly say my goodbyes and am racing to keep up with Chase as he practically drags me to his car. Once we are inside, it's as if the air has combusted with our lust and we immediately reach for each other. Hands everywhere, tongues clashing, breaths panting, our sole focus on being together. With too many people still around at the airport and Chase's having a small sports car, we manage to untangle ourselves for him to start the car and drive us to his condo.

"Layla, we are going to get into an accident if you keep touching me," he warns as my hands can't keep to themselves while he drives us at an accelerated speed. I remove my hands and try to calm down, wanting to savor every moment left with Chase. I look out the window as we drive into downtown, trying to memorize its beauty.

We reach his condo within fifteen minutes and Chase smoothly parks the car into his designated space. I notice he has his own private elevator and punches the button that leads to the penthouse. As soon as the doors close, he has me pushed against the wall, hands in my hair, consuming my lips with rough kisses that leave me breathless and aching between my legs.

All too soon the elevator doors open and we walk to his front door. He enters a number on the key pad and the doors unlock. I only get a brief glance at his massive foyer before he is leading us to his bedroom. He pulls me in and I gasp in awe at the gorgeous background of downtown Vancouver, its lights casting the perfect hue into Chase's bedroom. I walk toward the glass when Chase comes up behind, slides my trench coat off my arms and throws it onto a nearby chair. He moves my hair away from the nape of my neck and starts kissing his way up, his teeth grazing my earlobe which causes shivers to run down my spine. He spins me around and I stare up into his fervent eyes.

"I've never wanted someone as badly as I want you," he whispers as his finger traces along my bottom lip. His words make me clench my muscles in the promise of having him inside of me. My breathing has started to become shallow as my desire for him intensifies with his touch. I wrap my hands around his neck and bring his head down to my demanding lips. He starts to deepen our kiss, drugging my senses with the addiction that are his lips. His hands are roaming my ass, molding me to his body where I feel his erection bulging against his pants.

"Angel…I can't wait any longer. I have to be inside you, *now*!" He growls and we feverishly start to rip each others clothes off. He walks me backwards toward his bed, his lips never leaving mine. We only break apart when the back of my legs hit the bed, causing me to fall backwards onto it. The moonlight that enters his room enhances his muscular torso, causing my breath to hitch at the sight of his beautiful body. He watches me as my gaze follows his hands pushing down his boxers to reveal his hard cock. The sight of it in all its glory makes my mouth dry. I bite my lip to contain my moan of hunger to feel him inside of me.

He leans down over my body and takes one of my nipples into his hot, wet mouth. This time I do moan as his tongue starts thrusting against my bud, sending tingling sensations towards my core. He moves onto my other breast, giving it the same attention as he did the first one, while his hand roams down to my panties. His fingers move beneath the lace and soon his tongue and finger are in matching motions against my two sensitive areas. I ball the sheets into my fist, my head starting to thrash from the build-up he is causing inside me.

"Chase," I pant, not knowing how much more I can take of this. "I need you inside of me." He looks up from devouring my breast with a wicked grin and instead of answering my pleas, his mouth continues a hot path of destruction down my navel. When his mouth reaches the waistband of my panties, he uses his hands to quickly pull them down my hips and continues his assault with his mouth, but this time on my core. I start to pant louder, his tongue lavishing over my clit. My thighs instinctively start to tighten around his face as my climax is imminent.

"Chase...please," I whimper, his rotating tongue teasing me to the brink of no return. He stops as he feels my walls start to tighten. I groan from the loss of his touch and watch with hooded eyes as he meets my gaze with his own fiery one as he rolls the condom down his shaft. Never has the act of putting on a condom looked as seductive as Chase makes it look. As soon as he is finished, he grabs my hips to bring me to the edge of the bed, leans down into me and starts kissing me. When our tongues touching, he plunges inside of me. We moan into each other, the satisfaction of him being inside of me more than anything we anticipated. He slowly starts to thrust in and out of me, the friction making my walls clench around him.

"You feel so fucking amazing, Layla," he murmurs and stands up straighter. He positions my legs over his shoulders, grab onto my hips, and thrusts hard inside me. I gasp at the sensation of a little bit of pain mixed with so much pleasure and move my hands over his chest as he continues to thrust faster into me. My hands find his nipples and when I squeeze them, his moans get louder. I can see he is fighting against his release to make sure I cum as well. I reach down and start rubbing my clit in order to help. He watches our bodies become one and when he sees me start to play with myself, he tightens his hold on me and increases his speed. Between the friction of his cock inside of me and my finger rubbing against my clit, the dam holding back my orgasm completely bursts. My walls squeeze tightly around him as my screams of release fill the air. As I buck wildly against him, Chase's own release follows with an animalistic roar.

He falls against me, his body shuddering from the intensity of his release. Our chests are heaving as we gulp for air and I feel like I am floating from the incredible high he just brought me to. As tears of happiness silently slide down my cheeks, I wrap my legs and arms around him, holding onto him as tightly as I can. I close my eyes and memorize this moment as I never want to forget what he is making me feel.

He makes me feel alive again.

He makes my stomach do somersaults with just one glance.

He makes my heart pound in my chest with just one touch.

He lights me up from the inside with just one kiss.

He makes me forget about the pain of my past.

He gives me hope for my future.

Hope that I have found a home again with him.

27

CHASE

I wasn't expecting the ache I felt after dropping Layla off at the house this morning, but something shifted between us last night and the gravity of our situation weighs on me. If it was torturous leaving her today, I can't even begin to imagine how hard it will be tomorrow when she goes back to Chicago. I worshipped her body until the early hours of the morning, sleep only coming when our bodies finally gave out from exhaustion. We continued where we left off when we woke up, exploring each other in the shower before I took her to my favorite breakfast dive to satisfy our hunger pains.

I turn my phone back on, having turned it off so we wouldn't be disturbed last night, only to have missed messages from Rhys. I send him a short text saying I'm on my way into the office as I steer my car in that direction. My mind wanders back to Layla, the vision of her last night when we finally made love, forever engraved in my brain. I know she loves me - I felt and saw it in her eyes. I recall how she looked at breakfast this morning with her hair unruly from my hands and her lips swollen from my kisses. She looked even more gorgeous than normal, her face glowing with happiness. I want to make her that happy every day for the rest of my life. I almost told her I loved her, but held back as I am unsure if she is even ready to hear it, and I don't want to scare her away.

"Damn it!" I yell as I hit the steering wheel in frustration at the uncertainty of our future. I go over scenarios in my head on how to try to make a long distance relationship work with her. Would she be willing to move to Vancouver? Can I move permanently to Chicago and still do my job? But with the amount of time, energy, and traveling Wilson Enterprises is going to demand of me, I would barely see her whether she was here or me in Chicago. I can't negate my promise to my mother and brother on getting Wilson Enterprises back on its feet. I have to figure out a way to make this work because I am not going to lose her. By the time I arrive at the office, my mood has blackened and I have to shake the bitterness toward my father that rears it's ugly head at the situation he has put me in.

"You are late for your final fitting." Rhys arrives in my office no more than a minute after I cross the threshold. His handsome face is pinched tightly in irritation at my absence and his attitude toward me only heightens my anger.

"I know!" I bark out, glaring at him with irritation. "Considering we just got fitted for our tuxedos last week, I am sure it fits just fine."

"Why did you ignore my calls?" Rhys asks as he pushes himself off of the door frame and sits down in one of the chairs across from my desk.

"I was with Layla. Got a problem with that?" I ask, casting a murderous look in his direction to squash any objections he might have about it. His lips form a thin line and I can tell he is trying to choose his words wisely before speaking.

"She is quite a beautiful distraction, Chase. One that we cannot have at this moment. I need you here - mentally and physically."

"I promised you and Mother that I would honor my responsibilities as heir to Wilson Enterprises and I will fucking keep my promise!" I growl as I slam my fist against my desk in exasperation. Rhys' eyes widen slightly in surprise at my outburst. He nods in acknowledgement and stands up to leave.

"I will send the tailor in to see you," he says and walks out of my office to leave me alone with my dark mood.

Guests start arriving right on time for the private party we are throwing in Cal's honor. The venue we rented has unobstructed views of downtown Vancouver's waterfront, with the mountains providing a magnificent backdrop. We hired only the best caterer and florist to turn the venue into a formal garden and vineyard. Beautiful white flower vines hang from the ceiling, white portable walls filled from top to bottom with roses are alined along each corner for photography purposes. Grapes hanging off of vines are used as centerpieces for our guests to consume, food stations along the perimeter, and of course, bottles of Wilson Wine on every table. My mother, Rhys, and I start working the room, greeting and talking to the arriving guests. The invite list was purposely kept to a couple of hundred people, with our intention of inviting the elite businessmen and women of Vancouver and Canada in hopes to gain their interest in investing in Wilson Enterprises. The costs for this week have been exuberant, but will be well worth it if we can get a couple more investors to sign on the dotted line.

I look at my watch to see how much longer it will be until Layla arrives with Cal and Jenna. We specifically gave them an arrival time of one hour after the scheduled start time. With fifteen minutes left to spare, I make my way to Ellory and her family as her father is the next person on my list to recruit.

"When does training camp start for the Lynxes, Rhys?" I hear Roger Davis ask as they sit at a high top table near the dance floor, sipping on champagne. The Kelowna Lynxes are the last remaining sport steam we own and the team Rhys last played professional hockey for. He has been working closely with our general manager and our parent NHL team on what players will be on the roster for the upcoming season.

"Training camp starts in a couple of weeks. Hopefully, it will be an exciting season ending with us hoisting up the Calder Cup." Excitement lights up Rhys' eyes and I miss seeing his passion for the game.

I turn my attention to Ellory, wanting to catch up on how she has been doing when the words halt in my throat as I watch her look at Rhys. Raw passion radiates out of her brown eyes as she checks my brother out while he engages in conversation with her father. Ellory and I started dating when our father's forced us to spend time together during college. Our relationship quickly turned more into us becoming best friends and acting more like siblings than lovers. She has been a rock in my life, especially with the events surrounding my father. She would always tell me about the men she was dating, but she has never once mentioned her interest in Rhys.

How did I not know about this?

Does Rhys know?

Does Rhys feel the same way?

Commotion at the front entrance draws her attention away from Rhys and the moment is gone. She looks at me with a smile as we watch the arrival of Cal entering the main entrance.

"Looks like the guest of honor is here, which also means Layla has arrived," she says, enthusiastically as she throws an arm around my shoulders and squeezes. I give her a questioning look with a knowing smile, which causes her to narrow her eyes at me. "Why are you looking at me that way?" She questions.

"I think there is something you're not telling me. We are long overdue for a talk," I stand up and straighten my jacket to get ready to go and greet Cal.

"Yes, we are because you need to tell me what the plan is with

Layla!" She masterfully steps around my questioning to have the subject back on me.

"I have no plan. In fact, I have no idea what in the hell I am doing," I tell her. Rhys and I excuse ourselves from the group to head to the entrance. Cal is already working the room, shaking hands and introducing Jenna to people. She looks beautiful in a maroon dress with a metallic lace overlay that is fitted to her body, nude heels and her hair down in soft waves around her shoulders. Blonde hair catches my attention behind her and everyone fades away the moment Layla comes into full view. She looks stunning in a long black off the shoulder dress that has a heart shaped neckline with three quarter inch sleeves. The dress has a high slit that shows off her shapely left leg in high black heels. One side of her hair is pinned back with an elegant clip, while the other side is down with curls. She completely takes my breath away as images of her with her legs wrapped around me as I fuck her in that dress start to appear. I see her look around the party for me before she is greeted by Ellory, who manages to get to her before I can. I watch Ellory give her a hug, point to me, and maneuver Layla through the crowd toward me.

"Angel," I say as I shake my head in awe at her. "You look gorgeous." I wrap my arms around her and kiss her cheek. "I approve of this dress as it give me wonderful access to some of my favorite parts of you." I whisper in her ear as my hand grazes her exposed leg. Her cheeks are stained pink and she shivers as my fingers make their way underneath the fabric of her dress to her delectable ass.

"Behave, sir. You will get that later." She winks at me and my pants instantly feel tighter as my cock hardens. "This is quite the party," she says in appreciation as her eyes scan over the room. Suddenly her eyes bulge in shock at something she sees. "Who invited the wicked witch of the East?" she gasps and I follow her gaze as she is looking at none other than Cora Gregory. She is standing with Sean Lindsey, who is missing his usual charming smile. Instead he looks angry and is whispering something into her ear. But whatever he is saying to her has fallen on deaf ears as she is staring at Cal, watching his every move.

"You invited her here?" She questions as she stares at me incredulously.

"No, I didn't invite her. I have no idea who did," I confirm. Business wise, it would make perfect sense to try to sign her as a celebrity endorser. But I am a loyal type of guy and know how Jenna feels about her, so I won't even try to go there. Plus, there is something about Cora Gregory that gives me the wrong type of vibe. There is definitely more to her story than she lets on.

"I've got to go talk to Robert to see if he knows. Wait, where did he go?" She asks as she looks around the crowd to find Robert.

"I see him, but whose the guy he is with?" Robert is huddled close to a handsome black man in a navy suit, their heads so close together that it looks like they are about to kiss.

"That is Kellan, Cal's stylist, who dressed us all tonight and Robert's new obsession. Robert looks like he wants to eat him for dinner," she laughs as she leans in close to me and presses a soft kiss on my lips. I am pleasantly surprised by this gesture as I wasn't sure if she was ready for public displays of affection. "Let me go step into their sauna and cool them down." She winks at me and heads towards them.

As soon as Layla leaves me, Rhys swoops in to tell me we need to start the evening program. We start the program with speeches from my mother, myself and Cal, who introduces a short video of himself being interviewed and touring the vineyard. Three hours of schmoozing and talking with guests goes by before I have a moment to myself to try to find Layla. Cora is trying to talk to Cal, who only has eyes for Jenna as he watches her on the dance floor with Sean. Robert and Kellan are sitting close on one of the lounges, gossiping about the people they are watching. I look around in confusion as to why Layla is not with any of them. I walk past one of the rose walls when I finally see her head bent, talking to someone from a distance on the other side of the room. They are looking out the window at the incredible view of downtown Vancouver. It is only when she shifts on her high heeled feet that I recognize the other profile to be my brother. Anger starts to fill me as I notice his serious expression while talking to her. She nods her head at him while staring out the window with a look of complete and utter sadness. She responds back to him and his face registers surprise. He then takes her in his arms and hugs her, a gesture that is so rare for Rhys that it makes my steps falter as I approach them. Dread starts to seep through me as I know exactly what my brother is telling her to do.

He is telling her to let me go.

And she is going to do it.

I don't have to see the words come out of his mouth to know that is what he is implying to her. But for her to agree to do it is a knife to my heart. My brother sees me walking over to them and pulls away from her.

"Chase, I was just telling Layla about..." I don't give him a chance to continue as I punch him in the face, his body crumpling to the floor from the impact.

"Chase!" Layla screams as she kneels down next to Rhys to see if he is okay. Rhys looks up at me, blood trickling from his busted lip, hurt and confusion glaring through his eyes.

"What did you say to her, Rhys?" I yell, needing to hear those words come out of his mouth. "Why can't you be happy for me for once? Is this still punishment for Dad? For leaving you with the burden of the company? Tell me!"

"This is NOT the appropriate place for this," Rhys growls as he gets up off the floor. He looks around to see if anyone heard us, but fortunately, the band is playing at full volume, guests mingling and dancing, a wall of roses concealing our every movement. He looks between Layla and me and rakes his hand through his hair.

"I am not trying to punish you, Chase. I didn't tell Layla anything different from what she was already thinking." I look over at Layla, who looks down at her hands, her refusal to look me in the eye is all the confirmation I need.

"Layla, it was a pleasure meeting you and I hope you have a safe trip back to Chicago. Chase, I will see you at the office on Monday." Rhys holds the back of his hand to his lip and walks away.

I look over at Layla in disgust, more so with myself than with her. "So, that's what you came all this way for? A quick fuck to get out of your system so you can tell me goodbye." All this time I thought I could save her, make her see she is worthy at a second chance at love. But, she was never going to let me in. She chooses to stay scared over taking the risk of finding happiness again. I laugh bitterly at the irony that all this time I thought she was the one afraid of getting hurt, when in reality it is me who ends up getting shattered by her.

"Of course not, Chase. I was hoping that we could try being together, but these last couple of days have shown me how important it is for you to be here with your family. This is the real you! You thrive being the leader of Wilson Enterprises!"

"We can make it work, Layla. I will do whatever it takes to make us work. That is what airplanes are for, what the telephone is for. I will make the time for us to work, but you've got to do the same."

"Chase, I know we will eventually work, but I think we need to have some time to ourselves. You need to be fully vested here in your business and for your family. We won't work until we heal and we both have a lot of healing to do. You know you need to work on your relationship with your brother." She grips my arm, her eyes pleading with me to understand.

"That is for me to decide!" I yank my arm away from her, not being able to stomach her touch.

"If I was here, I would only be a distraction. You know that! You don't have time for me right now, Chase. And that is okay. Let's get ourselves where we need to be so we can have a healthy relationship together." She grabs my hand and squeezes it, holding on as tightly as she can. I look down at our adjoined hands, my eyes clouded with betrayal and anger.

"Relationship?" I laugh maliciously at her, wanting to hurt her as badly as she is hurting me right now. "Who is going to want to have a real relationship with you when you keep using your dead husband as an excuse for why you are damaged?" She flinches at my words and drops my hand.

"You accomplished what you set out to do, Chase. I fell in love with you." Tears are now streaming down her face, her words slashing at what is left of my heart. "But it is because I love you that I am choosing to let you go. I won't selfishly stand in the way of you working on being the best version of yourself that you can be." She picks up her purse off of the floor and stands back up.

"Goodbye, Chase." Her voice cracks with emotion as she looks at me one last time before departing.

She walks past me and out of my life.

And I let her.

28

LAYLA

Seven Months Later

I punch the code into the keypad to open the gate to Jenna and Cal's new house that they recently moved into. The gates slowly open and I drive my car through until I make it pass the gates, and then I watch as they fully close behind me before parking the car. The death threats against Jenna and Avery still continue, the FBI having zero leads on who could be behind them. Even though Cal has added a second bodyguard and they are living in a gated community with their own private gates and security cameras on the outside and inside of their house, I am still paranoid and always make sure I watch their gates close behind me without someone slipping in.

My cell phone starts to ring and I look at it to see that Emma, one of the assistants at work, is calling. Since I am ten minutes early, I decide to take the call in my car before going inside.

"Hey Layla, sorry to bother you on your day off, but Torrin has not arrived yet and his scheduled guests are here to tour the building," Emma says, and I close my eyes in irritation at him for once again being late to an important meeting.

"I'm sorry, Emma, but I am already in the suburbs. Can you do the tour, write down all of their needs, and I can draft up a proposal for them once I get to Los Angeles?" Cal and Jenna are taking us with them to the Academy Awards ceremony this weekend. It has been a busy awards season with Cal being nominated for Best Actor, but the Academy Awards are the most prestigious awards out of them all since it's your own peers nominating and voting for you. We are having our final dress fitting with Kellan and his staff before departing for the airport. Torrin is supposed to be going with me as my date, meeting us in Los Angeles Sunday morning since he's working to cover both of our shifts Friday and Saturday night, while I cover his shifts the following weekend.

Emma agrees to my plan and after we hang up, I immediately call Torrin. My call goes straight to voicemail and I don't even bother leaving a message. When I first started working at the House of Royalty, Torrin was the constant professional, showing me respect and treating me as an equal. He was an attentive boss, training me on every little detail on how to run the club and alternating closing nights with me to make sure I got a break. All the employees seemed to admire and respect Torrin, and he was very good at making sure everyone was taken care of and no one was overworked. We soon became friends and I didn't think twice about going to dinner with him or to the movies as that is what friends do. Three months into our new friendship, he said he wanted more.

At first I was resistant, saying I didn't think it was a good idea for us to date since we work with each other. I was working hard on bettering myself for once. I was working out daily, continuing to see my grief counselor, but I also started talking to a therapist as well. And even though Jenna lived farther away, she still met me every morning for our walks if she was in town. Life was starting to feel healthy, the only hiccup being that Torrin was not the man I wanted in my life.

Chase was, and I still to this day have not heard a word from him.

I left Vancouver brokenhearted, but knew my decision was the right one, even though Chase didn't see it that way. I reached out to Rhys one week after I had left, begging him to tell me how Chase was doing and to update me on his progress. The first couple of months were rough for Chase and it hurt to read Rhys' emails detailing the pain and anger Chase was going through. Chase, Rhys and their mother started to attend family therapy together when Chase and Rhys were not on the road promoting Wilson Enterprises and signing more investors and celebrity endorsers. But soon Rhys' emails started to become more positive. Chase was smiling and laughing more, and seemed less tense and stressed. Therapy was really helping them all resolve the bitterness and betrayal they felt against their father. Chase stopped his heavy drinking that he started the day I left and instead, was pouring all of his energy into the company. I thought with this change, I would start to hear from him again as surely he finally understood why I thought we needed to be apart.

I was wrong and he continued to stay radio silent.

In a moment of weakness from feeling rejected, I agreed to date Torrin. He took me to the fanciest of restaurants, lavished me with gifts, but when it was time to have sex with him, I couldn't do it. Robert thought I was crazy and should have my head examined, but despite Torrin's attentiveness and good looks, my heart ached for someone else.

And for once, it was not Charlie.

Chase still occupies my every waking thought and teases me in my dreams. Thoughts of what he was doing, if he was happy, if he was seeing someone else constantly consumed me. And even though Rhys always reassured me that Chase was still single, I had a hard time believing it.

Torrin was patient at first and said he would give me time. He continued to court me and I continued to enjoy having the companionship. But recently his behavior has been erratic and his mood swings have been intolerable. When I decided to finally introduce him to Cal and Jenna one night over dinner, he showed up completely incoherent. I was embarrassed and Jenna immediately hated him. Even though he has apologized and has tried to charm her, Jenna has not changed her stance on him.

She wants him completely out of my life.

Torrin's complicated behavior has started to affect his job. Missed client meetings and aggressive behavior has been reported to the owners of the club. The other employees and I tried to have an intervention with him and he played us like a fiddle, acknowledging that he needed to seek professional help and will do so. We saw glimpses of the old Torrin, but that only remained for a week.

It wasn't until I caught him snorting a line of cocaine in his office that I realized what was causing his Dr. Jekyll and Mr. Hyde personality. I couldn't understand how this once vibrant man, who prided himself in his looks by working out and eating clean, would put something so toxic in his body. I wanted to help save him from himself, so I let the outside world think we were still dating. I didn't want them to know his problem, so I created this facade in order for me to watch over him. He started to become my very own project, doing well when I was constantly with him, but not being strong enough to stop on his own. As I have learned from my own personal ordeal, no one can save you, but yourself. People can help you if you are open to it, but you have to want it.

And Torrin didn't want it.

He was too far down the rabbit hole of the high that cocaine gave him. I started to cover for him at work, but I have reached my limit and am done trying to take care of him. This weekend will be a last ditch effort and if there is still no willingness to check into rehab, then I will have to find another job, which I don't want to do. I love working at the House of Royalty. The staff became like a second family to me. I love being in control of their events and the owners have been impressed with the amount of revenue I have generated by bringing in outside corporate parties. Jenna and Robert have helped me a lot with this, even collaborating with us on by renting the venue out to use for their clients' parties. By not having to travel and living in Jenna's apartment, it has given me the chance to start fresh. I am strong, both mentally and physically, and haven't felt this way in a really long time.

I decide to send Torrin a text, telling him that Emma is covering for him, and to not miss his flight on Sunday. Surprisingly, he answers immediately, apologizes and says he is on his way to the office and that he promises not to miss his flight. I won't be surprised if he does, but I hope he proves me wrong.

I get out of my car, walk to the front door and punch in the key code. I enter their house, my nose immediately inhaling the scents of the essential oils that Jenna always diffuses. The house is beautiful, decorated in a Hollywood glam meets farmhouse chic kind of vibe. It boasts six bedrooms, offices for both Cal and Jenna, playroom for Avery, theater room, home gym and a pool. From the outside, the house looks massive, but the interior is laid out so that you don't feel like you would get lost. Everything is accessible, which was a requirement for Jenna as she didn't want to feel she could never find Avery. The house is bigger than Jenna wanted, but she fell in love with the backyard that has the pool, two outdoor living areas with a grill and outside seating, plus gorgeous landscaping. She already has had multiple photo shoots of themed parties staged outside in her backyard for her business' blog.

Voices lead me straight into the living room, where Jenna is standing on top of a portable platform with Kellan trying to zip up her dress around her hips. His expression is one of disdain as the zipper seems to not want to move. Jenna looks like she is about to cry. Cal is on the couch, observing her with heated eyes, while Robert is sitting on the lounge chair, typing on his computer.

"Jenna, that dress looks amazing on you," I say, announcing my arrival. I hug both Cal and Robert before plopping myself down on the couch to wait my turn. My eyes roam Jenna's body in a tight, rose gold sequin dress with an extremely low neck line and high leg slit that Cal has voiced his preference on for all of her formal dress attire. The sparkle of her dress highlights perfectly with the sparkler she is wearing on her left hand.

As soon as the director said "that's a wrap," Cal proposed to Jenna on the beaches of Phuket, Thailand, where she had zero hesitations and immediately said yes. A wedding date has been set for this fall, but they are currently arguing about the size of the wedding. Jenna wants a small, intimate ceremony with a big party, whereas Cal wants a big wedding, making sure everyone knows that she is his.

"How can this dress look amazing on her when I can't even zip it up!" Kellan exclaims in exasperation. "Jenna, we just let this dress out last week because of all the cheese that has been going to your ass! Please stop eating! We are now in crisis mode as the other dresses I have aren't acceptable. THIS is the dress for you!"

I watch Jenna swallow and quickly glance at Cal, who is looking at her in bemusement. Robert is staring at Kellan in lust, ready to pounce on him at any given second. The two have been together ever since Vancouver, each of them taking turns flying out to see the other since Kellan is based in Los Angeles. For right now, the long distance seems to be working for them both as they have hectic schedules during the week that require them to work long hours. Seeing them make their long distance relationship work makes me wonder if I gave up too easily on Chase. But Kellan and Robert do not have the demons that Chase and I have that we need to concur in order to be together.

"How does this happen with the amount of working out you do? I am sorry, but you have to go on a forty-eight hour cleanse in order to make this dress work." Kellan stands back to look at her with his hands on his hips, shaking his head in disapproval when he stops as Jenna bursts into tears. She covers her face with her hands in embarrassment, but can't stop her shoulders from shaking with her sobs.

"Oh, my God! No...please don't cry, Jenna. I didn't mean it! We don't have to do a cleanse if you don't want. Oh Jesus, Mary and Joseph, PLEASE stop crying!" Kellan glances between her and Cal, terror written all over his face. "You are still my second skinniest client. Oh, please stop! Cal, please don't fire me!"

Cal gets off the couch and wraps Jenna in his arms to comfort her. He murmurs something in her ear and she nods in agreement to whatever Cal said to her. I am watching this whole scene dumbfounded as the Jenna I know is not the type of person to cry over these kind of things. She would normally just shrug her shoulders and tell Kellan to kiss her ass, because she would never do a cleanse and would tell him to find another dress.

"I should fire your bloody ass for making my fiancée cry, but you're off the hook due to Jenna's raging hormones since she is getting deliciously plump from carrying my baby." Cal rubs her backside while looking at us with pure joy as excitement lights up his face.

"WHAT! You're pregnant?" I shout, jumping up from the couch and engulfing them in a hug. Robert runs to join us and we all squeeze each other, tears of happiness falling down our faces. Kellan has fallen to the floor in relief, his hand over his frantically pumping heart.

"Oh, thank you, Lord! When did you find this out and why didn't you tell me?" He asks as he sits up and looks over her in displeasure. Robert let's go and runs to the bathroom to get Jenna some tissues.

"I am officially thirteen weeks," she says, dabbing the wetness underneath her eyes with the tissue Robert hands her. "We wanted to wait a little bit longer, but I couldn't handle anymore comments on how large my ass has gotten from you." She wags her finger at Kellan, who starts to argue with her.

"First off, what the hell is thirteen weeks? I'm a man, I need months, not weeks!" She tells him that thirteen weeks is over four months, which seems to send him into a tizzy. "FOUR months! You have known you have been knocked up for four months and are *now* just telling me? I am the innocent one in this scenario, honey! This is all your fault! If you would have told me this sooner, I could have ordered the dress in a bigger size!" He throws his hands up in exasperation. "Now I am going to have to dress you in moos moos for the next however months you incubate that thing."

We all burst into laughter at the ridiculousness that is coming out of Kellan's mouth. As our laughter subsides, Cal announces we need to have a toast. He and Robert run into the kitchen and come back with four glass lutes filled with champagne and one filled with non-alcoholic sparkling apple cider for Jenna. We take our glasses and raise them in the air for his toast.

"To Jenna! Here's hoping for an easy pregnancy, a safe delivery for our healthy baby Harrington and to us for hopefully taking home the Oscar this weekend!" We all cheer, clink our glasses together and down our drinks in celebration.

I collect everyone's glass and walk them to the kitchen, needing a moment to collect my emotions. Despite my happiness for my friends, I can't help the sadness that creeps into my heart that Chase is not here with us celebrating.

"Layla, you're up next!" Kellan's voice breaks me out of my thoughts and I return to join them in getting ready for our weekend in Los Angeles.

29

CHASE

I stare out of my office window and watch as dusk settles in the background on the North Shore Mountains. This is one of my favorite times to be in the office, as it is quiet due to most of our employees already gone. I take this time to reflect on how things are going, the beauty of the sunset calming me from the hustle of the day.

Today was a big day for Wilson Enterprises as the first batch of bottled ice wine was exported. We were blessed with the perfect hard freeze this winter, which enabled us to produce a larger than normal production of wine. Due to our extensive marketing and advertising campaign featuring our celebrity endorsers, demand for ice wine was on the rise. We also were able to increase our radio and telecommunication coverage, courtesy of our newly signed investor, Roger Davis, which helped reach new customers. Because of the heightened visibility, our orders for ice wine were the highest in Wilson Enterprises history.

Our hockey team, the Kelowna Lynxes, are only six points away from clinching a spot in the Calder Cup Playoffs. Rhys has been working closely with their sales and marketing departments to increase advertising and promotions in order to sell out these last remaining home games that are left in the season.

There has been a buzz of excitement within the office these last couple of months. Employee morale is at an all time high due to the positive changes we have made for the company, which has included the importance of employee development.

Professionally, this has been one of the best years in my career, even more rewarding since Rhys and I were officially named co-CEOs of Wilson Enterprises.

Personally, this has been one of the worst years of my life.

I was spiraling out of control, trying to numb the pain of the loss of Layla with alcohol any chance I could get. I was physically present at the office, but was mentally unavailable. I was barely functioning and not making any headway in my personal relationship with my family or getting Wilson Enterprises back on track. One day, Ellory showed up at my office to take me to lunch, when in reality she drove me to the airport where my mother and brother were waiting to take me on a week long family therapy retreat in Salt Spring Island. That week of closing off the outside world and just hashing out our family problems kickstarted the journey to emotional wellness. We were able to have closure on the subject of my father and forgive one another for all the wrong doings and blame we had placed that stemmed from his actions. I left all of my emotional baggage that had my father's name on it on that island and haven't looked back since. When I do think about my father, I try to feel gratitude toward his hard work at setting up Wilson Enterprises in Canada and leaving that legacy to us.

Rhys and I have continued going to therapy to work on our relationship. We have forgiven each other for our past mistakes and have agreed to start on a fresh, clean slate. The change in each of us towards the other is night and day. Stoic, emotionless Rhys has not reared his ugly head in months. Instead, I have an energetic, enthusiastic partner in crime who is ready to conquer the business world with me. We are closer than ever, something I would never have imagined possible.

"I think Wilson Enterprises needs to step up our game and get back into the venue business," Rhys says, as he enters my office with a stack of papers, interrupting my quiet time.

"Depends on what venue you have in mind. If it is in a desirable location and we can keep it occupied, then it could be lucrative." I consider, remembering the times when we were successful in the past with our former venues before we had to sell them all in order to gain cash flow.

"I already have interest in a certain property." He throws down a stack of papers of what looks like to be a contract drawn up between Wilson Enterprises and Castle Entertainment, the owners of the House of Royalty night club. I look up at my brother in shock, my reaction only causing his smile to widen.

"It's time for you to go back to Chicago and claim what is yours, brother. Castle Entertainment was looking to sell and their lawyers have already reviewed the contract and are ready to sign."

I shake my head in surprise, not believing what my brother is suggesting. "She won't want me. I said some horrible things to her that night." Bile rises up in my throat as I recall the deplorable words I had said to her, despite her being right all along. I did need this time to be alone and work on me. If we did try to make long distance work, I don't know if I would be so far ahead with myself and how well we have Wilson Enterprises running. "Besides, she has already moved on to someone else," I say, with bitterness.

Three months ago I hired one of my old paparazzi buddies to follow Layla around. Despite the hurt and betrayal I had felt, I still missed her and wanted to know she was doing okay. I knew that it was probably a bad idea, but I thought it was worth the torture to just see her face one more time, even if it was in black and white photos. Nothing could have prepared me for the devastation I felt when seeing photographic evidence of her holding hands with Torrin Richards. I burned those photos, stopped having her followed, deleted all Google alerts on Cal and Jenna, and closed myself off from any mention or situation that would remind me of her, them and the city of Chicago.

"You, of all people, should know that pictures don't always portray reality. Read these in order and come find me when you are done." He hands me a file folder and walks out of my office.

I stare in confusion at the green folder before opening it up to reveal a stack of emails. I take a closer look and see that the email communication is between Layla and my brother, starting one week after she left. I can't help but to start reading, each page igniting the roller coaster ride of emotions in my heart. Betrayal, hurt, longing, wonder and finally, awareness. One hour later, I sit back in awe after reading her last email to Rhys, dated only four days ago with the news of Jenna's pregnancy and how her heart ached that I wasn't there with them to hear it. With Cal still being one of our investors, our staff was on cloud nine after hearing he won the Oscar for Best Actor and even had a congratulatory full page ad created to appear in a couple of major newspapers in Canada and the United States.

I should have been in Los Angeles with her.

These emails tell the story of the last seven months of our lives - hers from her perspective and mine from my brother's. It was difficult reading his earlier emails to her, detailing out my struggles. But reading them makes me proud of my accomplishments. I sighed in relief to read that she is not dating Torrin Richards, only trying to be his friend through a difficult time in his life.

I am amazed that Rhys managed to keep this a secret for so long. Two people who I care about developed a friendship, with the common denominated between the two of them being their love for me. Hope starts to fill me as I get up to go and talk to Rhys about what the implication of these emails mean.

All this time she has been inquiring about me.

All this time she has been missing me.

All this time she has still loved me.

"Rhys..." My voice cracks, thick with emotion and at a loss of words when I see him sitting at his desk. He stares at me for a brief moment, love and pride shining in his eyes. He recognizes my struggle to talk and holds up his hand.

"The acquisition of an existing night club is going to take some time to manifest to get up and running to our liking. Staff morale is going to be shaken up due to the changing of hands. It seems that an unspecified amount of time is going to be needed in Chicago." He clears his throat and tries to act serious, but he is having trouble containing the smile that keeps appearing on his lips. "Looking at the Lynxes' next away games, we conveniently play Chicago this Friday night. I have one available seat open on the team charter, but no available seating on the plane ride home. You will have to figure that out on your own once our new club is running to standards." He rises up, and moves around his desk to stand in front of me. "So, are we going to Chicago, Chase?" He asks with a knowing smile on his face.

"We are going to Chicago, Rhys!" I command in excitement.

"Well, then let's get this contract signed." He extends his hand for me to shake, but I surprise him by hugging him instead.

"Thank you for saving me...for saving us," I whisper and send a silent prayer of thanks for my incredibly strong baby brother.

30

LAYLA

It has been a long, tiring week since arriving home from Los Angeles and it is going to be an even longer weekend with the double I am working. Robert and I flew back Monday night while Cal and Jenna stayed since Cal had to do the obligatory press tour the following morning after his win. Knowing that Jenna is carrying his baby, only made the moment of him winning that gold figurine that much sweeter. Since both of their families came in for the monumental evening, they decided to stay longer to keep celebrating the win and the news of the baby by taking Avery to Disneyland. How I wish I could have stayed to see her excitement at seeing Mickey Mouse for the first time.

It was exhilarating being in Hollywood, seeing all those famous celebrities and watching Cal be recognized for the hard work he put into his movie. The only downfall of the trip was asking Torrin to come with me. He caught his flight Sunday morning and arrived at our hotel suite bright eyed and excited. We had lunch together and he acted like the old, charming Torrin that I knew and missed. I left him right after lunch to go get ready with Jenna, so I have no idea what he did to occupy his time while

I was gone. Once we were all in the limo heading to the Dolby Theatre, the new, coked up Torrin was in rare form. His words were flying out of his mouth a mile a minute, his pupils dilated and he couldn't stop sniffing. As soon as we were seated, he started fidgeting and stated he was going to the bathroom. He returned one hour later, completely drunk, and for the rest of the evening, talking about who he thought was hot and wanted to screw. I was relieved when as soon as we arrived at one of the after parties, Torrin headed straight for the bar and I didn't see him for the rest of the evening. Jenna was beyond furious and demanded that I leave him here to fend for himself. I had to tell her the truth about what was really going on with him, which in her eyes, didn't excuse his behavior.

When it was time to go back to the hotel, he was no where to be found. I left him multiple messages, all going straight to voice-mail. I barely slept that night, praying I would see him come through the hotel door at any minute. But when we arrived at the airport and Torrin wasn't at the departure gate, I then determined I was done trying to help him. I had covered for him at work, begged him to get treatment and even helped him the nights he was throwing up from any kind of withdrawal he was having. If he doesn't want to help himself, I can't do it for him.

I arrive at work and start preparing for my day to get ready for our usual rowdy Friday night crowd. The crowd will come early for happy hour, wanting to drink away the stress from their work week. I start every Friday morning counting inventory with our head bartender to order more liquor. Before I can even make it half way through, I receive a text from Torrin.

Torrin: Can you meet me in one hour?

Me: Glad to see you're alive, asshole! No, I can't. Some people have work to do.

Torrin: Layla, I really need to see you. I am headed to rehab for six weeks in Arizona. Please meet me!

I drop everything I was doing and meet him at Navy Pier.

He looked like shit when I arrived, sitting alone on one of the benches, looking out at Lake Michigan. His skin was ashen, his once beautiful eyes lifeless. His strong body seemed frail instead of sturdy. Tears start to well up in my eyes at the sight of him.

"Oh, Torrin!" I cry out as I plop down next to him, my eyes transfixed by his form. He smiles sadly at me and shakes his head.

"Yes, I look as good as I feel and from the reflection in your eyes, it is pretty shitty." He sighs and rubs his eyes to keep his own tears at bay. "I want to apologize to you for my behavior in Los Angeles. I was out of control and completely out of line. I hope one day you can forgive me." He looks down at his hands in shame, not able to meet my eyes.

I cover his hands with my own and squeeze. "I forgive you, Torrin. All I want for you to do is get better. I am proud of you for going to rehab."

"Don't be proud yet as I haven't proven anything to be proud of," he says, his voice filled with rejection.

"You can do it, Torrin. I have faith in you. Fight for yourself - you are worth it!" I repeat the words that so many people repeated to me in the past. It took me awhile to believe it, but I finally did. I hope Torrin will realize his worth sooner rather than what it took me to realize mine.

"The owners called me yesterday to let me know the club has been sold to new ownership. They didn't say who, but for us to not be surprised if they just pop in one day soon." This news comes as a surprise as I didn't realize the owners were wanting to sell the club.

"I put in my letter of resignation and asked them to forward it onto the new owners. I also wrote up a letter of recommendation for you to be promoted to the new General Manager." My head shoots up in surprise at his news. I am the rookie on the staff and don't feel the promotion would be justifiable.

"Torrin, thank you, but I have only been there for close to eight months. I don't deserve to be promoted yet!"

"You're a leader, Layla. Everyone sees that. They respect and enjoy working with you. You treat everyone as an equal and make sure they are all taken care of. You would make a wonderful General Manager." He smiles at me while pushing a piece of wind blown hair behind my ears.

"I learned from the best, Torrin," I softly say as I brush away the lone tear that has fallen down my cheek.

He stares at me for a couple more seconds before standing up, indicating he is ready to leave.

"I have a plane to catch. Take care of yourself, Layla. Stay safe and I truly hope you find happiness and love again." He pulls me to him and wraps me tightly in a hug. I hold on as long as I can before he lets me go and walks away.

As soon as I got back to the club, I called an emergency team meeting and told the staff the news about the new ownership and Torrin. Everyone was in shock - some started crying, others agreed he needed to go. Everyone had questions about the new ownership and I promised them I would get details as soon as I could. With the club opening up in three hours, a lot of things still needed to be accomplished and we all worked as a team to make it happen.

Once the club opened, I stayed on the floor for the first two hours, observing the crowd control at the bar and the dance floor, checking upon the waitresses, bartenders, DJ and bouncers. When I felt we were in our routine flow for the evening, I went back up to my office to decompress and to check to see if I had any emails with information on who the new owners might be and how I could reach them.

The shrill of ringing from my office phone disrupts me and I answer it immediately to make sure we don't have any problems on the floor.

"Layla, a man claiming he is the new owner has arrived. Do you want me to escort him upstairs?" Emma asks, her voice barely audible over the thumping of the house music.

Shit, shit, shit, why do they have to show up tonight!

"Yes, please!" I shout into the phone in order for her to hear me. I quickly hang up and pull out the makeup bag I keep in my desk drawer for the times I work closing. I pull out a compact mirror and groan as I view the bags underneath my eyes and the remnants of my eye shadow barely still on. I quickly apply more blush and lipsticks before throwing everything back in my draw when a knock sounds on my door.

The door starts to open and I walk around my desk to greet Emma and our new owner, when my breath whooshes out of my lungs and I stop dead in my tracks, astonished at the sight of Chase Wilson standing in my office.

My eyes roam over his face, noticing his Adam's apple bobbing up and down as he swallows in nervousness. He studies me, a flicker of hesitation crossing those turbulent eyes before they clear. Gone is the hatred that was in them the last time I saw him. Instead there is something else. Something I have seen before. Something I have been dreaming about.

Desire.

Chase Wilson still desires me.

"Layla, this is Chase Wilson with Wilson Enterprises. He says he is the new owner and seems to have brought with him a signed contract to prove it." Emma tries to hand me the contract, but I am immobilized at the sight of him. He looks thinner in the face and in his frame, but it does nothing to diminish the sex appeal that ripples off of him. His hair is longer, styled to his jawline. He hides that insatiable body of his in a two piece navy blue suit, silver shirt and tan dress shoes with matching belt. He is the most beautiful man I have ever laid eyes on.

"Layla, are you okay?" Emma questions, giving me a worried look as she glances between me and Chase.

"I'm sorry, yes...yes, I'm fine." I try to shake away the trance I am in at seeing him here. I ball my hands into fists, wanting to feel the pain of my nails digging into my flesh so I know I am not dreaming. I extend my hand out to him, needing to feel his touch. "It's nice to meet you, Mr. Wilson." The sexy smile he gives back undoes me and it takes every ounce of will power not to fling myself at him in front of Emma.

"The pleasure is all mine, Ms. Sands." His husky voice draws my attention to his soft lips. My core starts tingling as it remembers what those lips have done to me, how they made me feel and how I want more. He grabs my hand and squeezes, the electricity from his touch making me gasp out loud.

Emma looks even more baffled at my reaction to him and decides to take her leave. "I am needed back downstairs. I will leave you two alone to discuss things. Layla, please call me if you need anything." I ignore the worried tone in her voice and faintly hear her footsteps retreat, the door finally closing with a loud click.

We continue to stare at each other, both of us not knowing what to say, but needing to say everything. He is here and I don't know for how long, so I swallow my fear as this is a now or never moment for us.

"You didn't have to buy a nightclub in order to come see me," I tease, needing the mood to be less intense. He turns slowly and walks back to the door. I am about to object to his departure when I hear the turn of the lock. He turns back around, his stride slow and purposeful as he makes his way toward me. His gaze is hungry and I am more than ready to feed his appetite.

"I bought this place because you told Rhys in one of your emails that you loved it here." My eyes grow wide with the acknowledgement that he knows about our communication. He stops right in front of me, inches away from touching me, but yet keeping his hands to himself. My heart is screaming at me to make the first move, to show him I am ready if he is, but my body stays paralyzed.

"If this place makes you happy, then I want to be here with you. The time has come for us, Layla. It is time for me to fulfill every single one of your desires for the rest of our lives."

My mouth drops open and that is all it takes for him to swoop in and crush me to him. Our lips meet and I swear it feels like an inferno, the heat we have for each other ready to combust. His tongue invades my mouth and I moan at how good he tastes; how good he feels. Our hands roam all over our bodies, grabbing and needing, ravenous for each other's touch. Soon we start taking each other's clothes off, our fingers not moving fast enough as we start ripping and pulling the barriers off, the need to be flesh on flesh too great. He has my senses on overload and all I can comprehend is my want of him inside me.

"I am so sorry, Layla," he groans in between his searing kisses. "I am sorry for the pain I have put you through all these months. You were right that I needed time to myself. You were right and I was too stubborn to realize it because all I wanted was you." He stops kissing me and touches his forehead to mine, giving us a chance to catch our breaths.

"That's the past, Chase. All the matters is that you are here now." I touch his face with my hands and make him look into my eyes. "I love you, Chase." I bring his lips back to mine so I can show him how much I love him, not caring that I am at work in a building filled with hundreds of people.

He lifts me up and I wrap my legs around his waist, grinding myself on his erection as he walks us back to my desk. He sets me down, our hands pushing items off the desk, not caring if anything breaks, in order to make room as our mouths are still fused together. He grabs my thong at the sides of my hips and pulls it down over my legs. He starts playing with my clit with his finger, distracting me as I unbuckle his belt and unzip his pants. I maneuver his pants down his hips and cup his dick, which springs to life from my touch.

"I'm sorry, Angel, but I just can't wait anymore." He lays me down, his Adonis like body hovering over me as he quickly thrusts inside of me. Our bodies shudder, our moans of satisfaction loud at the intensity of him finally being back inside of me. He starts to move faster, the desk moving to the rhythm of our bodies. But soon we can't control the desk from sliding out from underneath me, so he carries me to the couch, never once pulling out of me. He slowly sits down in order to not hurt me and leans back against the couch, bringing me with him which causes him to be deeper inside of me. I move my hips back and forth against him, the sensations of me being on top of him too much to bear and I start to ride him. I ride him hard and fast, our greed to satiate each other overwhelming. With my orgasm ready to explode, I break our kiss to scream out my release as I continue to bounce on top of him, my walls squeezing as tightly as I can at the same time he yells out my name in his own release.

He crushes me to him, his arms locking around me as we pant out our breaths from our incredible high of love making. I wrap my arms around his neck, every limb of my body now wrapped around his and I inhale his scent that I have come to love.

The scent that I recognize as home.

"I'm never letting you go again, Angel," he murmurs as we feel our hearts beating against each other's chest.

"You will never have too, as I am yours." I promise and seal it with a kiss.

EPILOGUE

LAYLA

Three Months Later

I rub my feet against the soft grass as I look up at the sky to soak in the sunshine. It's another beautiful day in Chicago, with no clouds in the sky. I sigh in contentment, grateful that there is no rain for today.

"Do you always order up beautiful weather for me when I am with you, Charlie?" I ask his headstone as I sit for my annual visit on the anniversary of his death. It is the first I've spoken in the ten minutes I have been here so far. I always just sit here and observe the scenery first upon arrival. Normally my mood is bleak and depressed. But life has been wonderful these last three months with Chase by my side.

The House of Royalty is thriving under the ownership of Wilson Enterprises. With Chase's marketing skills, we have become busier, hosting a record number of events. Due to our demand, we had to double our staff and made the necessary renovations needed to keep the club in the status of one of the most sought out venues in Chicago.

Working with Chase has been easy - getting to go home with

Chase every night has been a dream. He makes me happier in ways I could never imagined possible and I am grateful each and every day with my second chance at love, at happiness. I look behind my shoulder to see him waiting for me. He has taken Jenna's place by accompanying me on my visit, but being respectful of my time alone. He sees me looking at him and he smiles as he blows me a kiss. I give him a thumbs up, indicating that I am doing okay, before turning my attention back to Charlie's grave.

"Life sure is different from one year ago. I am proud of myself and I know you are too." I continue on with honesty, not feeling guilty anymore for loving someone else other than him. "He makes me happy, Charlie. So incredibly happy. But you always wanted this kind of life for me. I am sorry it took me so long to want it for myself," I sigh, trying hard to not have any regrets at how long this journey has been for me. But if I wanted it for myself sooner, who knows if Chase would have come into my life.

"We have to go back to Vancouver soon to start the new ice wine harvest, but I promise you that I will always be back to see you." Chase and I have agreed that we will split up the year between our two cities - six months in Vancouver and six months in Chicago. It will be a big transition for me, but with Chase by my side, I will be just fine.

I look around the cemetery one last time, deciding that it is time to go. We are all on borrowed time and I now would rather spend all of that time with Chase and the rest of people who love me.

"I have to go, Charlie, but I know you will always be with me." I keep my normal ritual of kissing the grass before I stand up to depart. I take one long look at his headstone before exhaling, not realizing I was holding my breath.

"I love you, Charlie. Always and forever." I turn around and walk away from my past and into the awaiting arms of my future.

ACKNOWLEDGMENTS

Hi Friends! I truly hope you enjoyed Layla and Chase's story. It was not an easy story to tell, but aren't we so happy that they both got their happily ever after?

The first thank you needs to go to you, the readers, and the bloggers. Thank you so much for your positive feedback, love and support. Thank you to the bloggers who work long hours to help advertise and support us authors.

Thank you to my family, especially my husband and children. Without their support, I wouldn't be able to continue living my dream.

Thank you to Erica, Rachel, Crystal and Neil for your continued support, especially when I torture you with my whining when I don't feel the story in my head is ever good enough.

Thank you to Najla, Emma, Cissie and Shelly who helped design and edit this book.

Thank you to my Misfits for your continued support and promotion of my books!

Sean Lindsey's story will be up next in Edge of Desire, book 3 of the Let Me In series. I can't wait to share it with you! Please make sure you follow me on all of my social media pages and sign up for my newsletter at authorjessicamarin.com to be up to date with upcoming releases and book signings.

Peace and love,

Jessica

ABOUT THE AUTHOR

Jessica Marin began her love affair with books at a young age from the encouragement of her Grandma Shirley. She has always dreamed of being an author and finally made her dreams of writing happily ever after stories a reality. She currently resides in Tennessee with her husband, children and fur babies. When she is not hanging out with her family, she loves watching a good movie, going dancing with the ladies, sniffing essential oils and daydreaming of warm beaches, winning the lotto and world peace.

Jessica would love for you to join her on all of her available social media outlets.

10837635R00124

Made in the USA
Lexington, KY
01 October 2018